THE RAJAH FROM HELL

H. BEDFORD-JONES

THE THUNDERBOLT OF INDRA

THE COMPLETE CRIMES OF THE RAJAH FROM HELL

H. BEDFORD-JONES

ILLUSTRATED BY
JAMES A. ERNST

COVER BY
CHARLES WOOD

STEEGER BOOKS • 2020

TABLE OF CONTENTS

THE THUNDERBOLT OF INDRA

Four prominent men were marked for murder. Here
follows the fascinating story of the first strange case.

IN JUNE, a Congressional bill opened the immigration
door to a quota of one hundred natives of India per year.
Some of the English were clearing out of India about this time,
too. It was in August that I was invalided home, and stepped
into the result of these political doings when my ship tied up at
Los Angeles harbor. The result was murder, deviltry let loose;
and I was in the middle of it.

For the first time in seven long years, I set foot again on
American soil, with the war over and almost forgotten. Here I
was a mere nobody—just another doctor, one white-collar man
among thousands competing for work: Hugh Clements, M.D.,
looking for a job.

Back in India, this same Hugh Clements had been a person
of importance, the master of a mission hospital, the petty lord
of a district, hobnobbing with the great, clubbing with judges,
rajahs, noblemen, soldiers. Here he was a man of thirty-two,
unknown and obscure—or so I thought. Yet none of us can
escape the backwash of the past. Here, far away from India, the
relentless shadows of that bloodstained country were reaching
out to cloud my path with mystery and appalling horror.

Even aboard ship the thing began. Just before we docked, I
received a rather curt radiogram which astonished and delighted
me:

Hugh Clements, M.D.
S.S. *Island Queen*

Immediately you arrive telephone me Hotel Vista, Pasadena.
Urgent and imperative. Best regards.

Trent.

Astonishing as were the brusque words, they were character-
istic of the signer. Sir James Trent, the judicial light of my Indian
district, was a typical British jurist; conservative and dignified,
yet delightfully human. I had been much with the family.

Six months before I started home, Trent left India on sick
leave, taking his daughter Virginia with him, and stopped in
California under medical care. I had naturally written them of
my coming arrival, but had received no response. Hence, the
radiogram was heart-warming. So was the thought of seeing
Virginia so soon.

Trent held me in a certain annoyed respect because of my
propensity to cut red tape and get brisk results. Also, I knew
India far better than he did, for my father had had an American
hospital there in past years. I had pulled Trent's charming and
lovely daughter through two bad fever attacks, and we were on
a basis of firm friendship, at least. His "urgent and important"
summons rather baffled me, but I had no premonitions, merely
very pleasant anticipations. Murder was far from my thoughts.

So, upon disembarking, I sought out the "C" section of the
Customs shed. No one was meeting me, I had no relatives
to bother about and was pleasantly unhurried. The day was
young, and I took an eager delight in the American scene. It
was wonderful to be among my own people once more. I found
my trunks, lighted a cigarette, stood waiting for an inspector to
attend to me, and thought what a lucky devil Hugh Clements
was to be out of India forever.

"I have a room for you at my hotel, the Armitage." Spoken
in Hindustani, from close behind me! It was a man's voice, a
peculiar voice, so powerful and richly vibrant as to set the spinal
nerves tingling. And—in Hindustani! "We can get a doctor
there. If necessary, I can telephone and get one now."

"I can wait, Your Highness," came a feeble, thin response. "But

I know the feeling. An attack is coming on."

Partly from curiosity, partly from professional interest, I turned and looked at the speakers. They were quite close to me, beside two large trunks.

The one was an old man with waxen skin, quite bent and feeble, whom I had several times seen aboard ship, always alone, always

I found that the envelope contained ten crisp one-hundred-dollar bills.

occupying a deck-chair, obviously an invalid—and as obviously a white man. His name was Chaffee, and this was the only thing I knew about him.

But the other—the "Highness" who must have come to meet him here, the man of striking voice, was startlingly handsome. He had a faintly bronze skin, a thin black mustache, and wonderfully powerful, magnetic eyes; he was the sort of man who dominates whatever company he may be in—young and aggressive and vital. I took him to be a Hindu or perhaps a Rajput. His business suit was excellently tailored. In his necktie was an old-fashioned scarfpin, a most unusual jewel, an intensely black stone that held a glowing crimson flame.

"I beg your pardon." I spoke impulsively, also in Hindustani to explain my intrusion. "If you are in need of any help, I happen to be a doctor."

The younger man turned to me. His dark, luminous eyes suddenly flashed as though in recognition. Indeed, to my great astonishment, he greeted me by name.

"Is it possible? Why, you're Dr. Clements, from the Gyantse Memorial Hospital at Lacpore!"

I smiled. The name was lettered large upon my trunks, of course.

"Correct, though I don't think we've ever met."

This seemed to amuse him.

"Well, since you don't recognize me, naturally you don't know me," he said. "Thank you for the offer. If we have any need, we shall be glad to call you in, but at the moment there's no necessity. May I have your address?"

"I have a reservation at your own hotel, the Armitage," I said rather curtly. The way he spoke, his discourtesy in withholding his name nettled me. At this instant an inspector arrived, and nothing more passed between us. The two men had finished and departed long before I had my luggage clear.

Yet the timbre of that unknown man's voice lingered with me, quickening my pulses like the echoes of a rich temple bell. It was vibrant with force of character—that singular quality few can explain, which makes many an actor great, and enables even untrained talent to capture a crowd. Chaffee, I rightly concluded, was old and failing and of small importance, but his companion might be someone in Hollywood's acting circle. Good God, to think what a sorry stab at the truth I made!

Upon getting to the hotel and reaching my room, I put in a call for the hotel in Pasadena, and not upon Trent's account either. Still, I had no claims upon his daughter, merely a hope. At length I heard the rasping English voice of Sir James. He greeted me with a hearty cordiality that was good to hear.

"Your radio message was a bit laconic," I observed. "Nothing wrong, I trust?"

"Nerves, my boy, merely nerves. I was devilish upset when I sent that message, but everything's right now. Virginia is looking forward to seeing you, no less than I am. Can you drop in on us for tea?"

"Whenever you say, of course."

"We're just leaving for a luncheon engagement. Suppose you come over about four, Clements, if you will."

"On the dot," I rejoined, and hung up.

Why had he previously been so upset—why was everything now all right? And why had not Virginia been the one to answer the phone, dammit? No use asking myself silly questions, though.

So I devoted myself to unpacking and getting settled, since I expected to be at the hotel for the next week or two. Twelve-thirty saw me in shape, and I was on the point of seeking luncheon when my telephone rang. Answering, I immediately recognized the vibrant tones of Chaffee's companion.

"Dr. Clements? I am taking advantage of your kind offer of help. Will you be good enough to come to Room Five-Ten? It is urgent."

"I'll be right along," was my reply. I paused, however, to phone the desk and inquire who had Room 510. A Mr. Chaffee, was the reply—Howard Chaffee.

I was curious, of course. Unknown as he was to me, that younger man exerted a singular fascination. A Hindu? Impossible to say. His English had an Oxford intonation. So I hurried; when I knocked at the door in question, the man himself opened to me. I perceived that this was not a single room but an entire suite.

"I'm thankful you're here; it's my elderly friend Chaffee," he said rapidly. "The hotel doctor has proven quite useless; my own efforts are useless. You must see what you can do. Chaffee is subject to a spasmodic contraction of nerves and muscles. He can assign no reason, and no physical cause is discernible. I should tell you that until quite recently he has been in Tibet for a long time."

"My hospital was at Tibet's back door," I said. "Where is he?"

Chaffee was in the bedroom, unconscious and breathing stertorously. I made a swift examination. Somewhat to my surprise, his body told me that he was not nearly so old as he

had appeared. But the scars—the scars! They horrified me with
their evidence of repeated tortures; and at the same time, they
informed me of everything. During the long war years I had seen
such scars more than once. Northern India had been ranged by
spies and secret agents of a dozen nations in those days; cruelty
had run rampant.

I looked up, to find the younger man watching me with
anxious attention.

"This is no case for medicine," I told him abruptly. "We have
here an affection of the motor nerves, caused by certain positions in which the man has been tied for long periods. It's a
rather ghastly form of punishment or torture used in Tibet.
I've encountered it several times. There's no cure, I'm afraid. The
trouble is progressive."

"So he has informed me." My host regarded me calmly—it
was the calm, not of unconcern, but of complete concentration
upon me. "Can you give him any relief?"

*There was nothing
to indicate who had
caused it or what had
happened. But Sir
James Trent was dead.*

"Temporary relief, yes, but the attacks will recur. If you'll watch, I'll show you what to do in future crises of this kind."

I took off my coat and turned the unconscious, stiffened figure of Chaffee on its face. Then, during a good twenty minutes, I kneaded the nerve ganglia along the spine and at the base of the skull, to restore the lost circulation and stimulate the atrophied or dying nerves. I explained the process as I continued it.

At length the old chap uttered a gasp, and made a slight movement. I turned him over again. He was conscious now; he smiled up at us—a feeble, kindly smile—and then closed his eyes and was asleep on the spot.

Donning my coat, I followed the younger man into the outer room there he turned and regarded me fixedly. His manner was most peculiar. His features were like golden-brown stone, impassive and without thought or emotion behind them; yet in those depths stirred a more profound thought, a more acute emotion, than I would have deemed possible. I was dimly aware of this at the moment, yet only dimly.

"Forgive me for not mentioning my name; it is of no consequence," he said. "I must remind you of something far more important, something that happened three years ago. You were walking along a street in Lacpore and encountered a poor devil, out of his head, at the very point of death. Nobody cared; but you did. You took him into your hospital and restored him to life."

His knowledge startled me; he was calm, inscrutable, impervious. I lit a cigarette and nodded at him, wondering how he could have heard of the incident.

"Yes, I recall the case. A poor chap—a young fellow, too— badly injured in some native feud; shot up, wasn't he? Wounds festering, body emaciated, brain in delirium. I remember that one night, later, he completely vanished. I never learned who he was or what became of him. Odd that you should have heard of the mystery."

"Odd? No. He was a friend of mine. And now that man is dead," he replied. A sudden flash of terrific inward radiance leaped into his eyes and then was gone again—as though a furnace door had opened and closed. He extended an envelope to me.

"The kindness you did him, Dr. Clements, is not forgotten; take this, with my earnest thanks. I am one of those unfortunate people who never forgive an injury and who never forget a kindness. Goodbye. It was kind of you to give your help with poor Chaffee."

He almost pushed me out of the suite, clearly desiring no further discussion of that happening in Lacpore.

When I reached my own room and opened the envelope, I found that it contained ten crisp one hundred dollar bills.

Those eyes of his haunted me. Despite his words, I was tempted to think that this handsome, wealthy man might be the poor devil of a native I had picked up in the street. The notion was impossible and fantastic, and I dismissed it. And who was this white man from Tibet, this Howard Chaffee, so scarred and doomed by old tortures?

Behind those two men in Room 510 I sensed some titanic story, and my intuition was more frightfully correct than I dreamed. However, at the moment I chucked up the whole affair as one of those singular incidents cropping up in every physician's life. The war years, particularly in Asia, gave birth to many queer happenings.

So the matter was closed, I reckoned, and gratifyingly so; that thousand-dollar fee was badly needed. When I went downtown after lunch, I turned the money in with my other funds at the bank, and accounted myself lucky. Seldom do such sums bob up from the forgotten past!

Slightly before four o'clock a taxicab took me across the famed old Pasadena "suicide bridge," as the newspapers call that lofty structure from which so many unhappy souls have dropped to oblivion. Perhaps it was an ominous and sinister omen, but I quite forgot it in my anticipation of seeing Virginia Trent again.

I left the cab in the flowering grounds of the hotel, dotted by guest cottages in every direction. I went straight to the main building, and as I entered, came face to face with Virginia herself, to our mutual surprise.

What a lovely girl she was! Delicately slim and slender, so poised, so cool and sensible; violet eyes, bronze masses of hair, a skin like rosy gold. The sincere delight in her greeting flung me off balance and set my pulses hammering. We stood talking eagerly—would we had not! A moment or two might have made such a difference!

At length I asked after her father, and she broke into a laugh.

"Oh, I forgot that you really came to see him, Hugh! He's as well as can be expected; he banished me from the cottage half an hour ago. He's writing his memoirs, you see—'Bygone Days in the Punjab' or some such poisonous title. Who cares about bygone times these days? The atomic age has put the past out of mind. But he's enjoying it all, whether anyone else does or not."

She sobered, as I made some light comment, and looked me in the eyes.

"I must warn you, Hugh: he'll not be with us long. A few months at most, I'm afraid. But come along and see him for yourself. You might take a hand in his treatment; I've more faith in you than in any other doctor I know."

"He said over the phone he'd been upset," I mentioned. We had turned out of the main building and were strolling through the grounds toward the cottage occupied by the Trents.

She nodded.

"Yes, a bad thing happened yesterday. He got a letter, but burned it at once and refused to discuss it. His nerves have been ragged ever since."

A MOMENT later we walked into the cottage, Virginia giving her father a cheery hail. But there was no answer. We found him fallen forward across his writing table, found him suddenly and horribly murdered, and within a matter of minutes.

Some unknown, pointed weapon had struck him over the temple, making one deadly wound and four slight ones surrounding it. There was absolutely nothing in sight to explain the hurt; there was nothing to indicate who had caused it or what had happened. But Sir James Trent was dead.

Within five minutes the phone brought two radio cars. Commotion was held down to a minimum, but within the cottage was a furious rush of details, interviews, and police investigation. Virginia went to pieces. It was lucky that I had arrived in time to help her in these matters and to shield her from impertinent curiosity.

The hotel management came forward handsomely, assigning Virginia another cottage and against her protest providing a nurse to accompany her to it. When the ordeal of questioning was over, I helped pack up her things for the move, and saw her to her new quarters with the nurse, a woman almost as young as herself.

I had another go at the police. They gave me no information—could not, in fact, as they had none themselves and were obviously mystified. The only person who displayed any gumption was the hotel physician. He beckoned me aside and took me to his own office. He had heard a bit about me from Sir James, he said, and provided a drink. Then he regarded me with curious interest.

"Did you examine that wound, Clements?"

I nodded. "Yes. I don't savvy it at all. An inch deep and round, as though made by the end of a poker; but there's no poker about the cottage. And those four marks around the wound, too!"

"Right," he assented gravely. "Barely breaking the skin. As though there were four blunt pokers around the central sharp one that pierced to the brain. I thought you might know of some Indian weapon which could produce such a wound."

"Absolutely none," I replied, "and there's nothing on the place to have caused it. The police are stumped. So am I. No robbery, nothing taken, either. Why the murder? No cause. Have you any East Indians on the premises?"

"Nary a one. No Hindus around here, except the Hollywood

"I have a room for you at my hotel."
It was a man's voice—in Hindustani.
"We can get a doctor there."

fortune-tellers, and they are probably fakes. The check-up shows that Sir James had no visitors this afternoon. His daughter knows of no enemy."

"Yet somebody slipped in and killed him," I said.

He assented. "Yes. But the weapon—what could it have been? If we knew, it might give us a direct lead, might tell us everything. The police are confused; they'll get nowhere."

The hotel manager interrupted us, seeking me. A gentleman was in the lobby, a friend of Sir James—would I see him? A Colonel Magruder. At the name, I came out of my chair like a shot. Magruder! Why, he had retired, had left India a year ago to go home to Scotland. What was he doing here, if this was the same man?

It was Colonel Angus Magruder and no other. Trim, precise, lantern-jawed, a pure martinet, and even in his civvies an obvious soldier. He wrung my hand hard, and we retired to the easy chairs in one corner of the lobby. He had of course heard what had happened, and the news had put him into deep agitation.

"A frightful affair, Clements!" he exclaimed. "Trent asked me over for tea to see you again. I'm living in Hollywood, you know. My niece is an actress in the cinemas there."

"All news to me," I said. "I supposed you were in Scotland."

"I was, for a bit, then came over here to be with my niece—but I say, Clements! When I first got here I heard about this affair, but don't half recall what they told me—it gave me a terrible turn. Have they found the chap Ram Lal? Trent had a chit from him yesterday, threatening us both—"

I leaped out of my chair. "Good Lord—that letter! Then you know who killed Trent?"

"No, no—that is to say, I thought you were aware of it. He intended to talk it over with you," said Magruder, mopping his forehead. Luckily, we were quite alone and no one witnessed my excited conduct. The newspapermen had all departed. "He phoned me, telling about the letter. It would be no proof as to the murderer, I imagine—but confound it all—"

I cut in upon his incoherence.

"Magruder, if you know anything definite, let's have it. Trent was found dead and not a soul knows anything about it. Virginia said he had received a letter but burned it and refused to discuss the matter."

"Burned it? Then, dash it all, the evidence is gone!" Magruder stared at me. "Here, sit down; you make me devilish nervous. I'll tell you what it's all about."

To him, the shock had been terrific. He produced a cheroot and bit at it; his firm hand was unsteady. When he spoke, he picked his words with care.

"Some years ago we sent a dacoit—a hill bandit—to prison for life. Ram Lal was the name—ordinary name, ordinary banditry. Yet the case made quite a stir. You may remember it."

I shook my head impatiently, wondering what he was driving at.

"I brought the beggar in, by a bit of luck," he resumed. "Trent sentenced him. Balfour—he has retired since that time—prosecuted the chap; rather brilliantly done, too, since the evidence was not at all conclusive. I should mention that I was enabled to catch the fellow through information given us by an American teak-buyer whom this same Ram Lal had held for ransom. That made four of us, counting the American, you see; four of us vitally concerned in the matter. Four of us did it."

HIS MANNER startled me profoundly. He was badly frightened. In such a man as Magruder, to whom fear seemed an utter stranger, this was a singular thing.

"Well, he made the usual threats bitter ones, too," Magruder went on uneasily. "The war came along. He escaped, and turned up in Moscow. He came back to India at the time of the food riots, was in the Bengal affair, and the police finished him. Put half a dozen bullets in him. I heard. His Communist friends got him away but he died in the jungle somewhere—or so it was said. That's one angle of the business."

He paused to eye his cigar thoughtfully then shot me a sudden, almost furtive glance; perhaps he was not too proud of the story he was telling.

"Later it came out that this chap was no ordinary native. He was the nephew of the Rajah of Sirvath: and today he'd be on the throne. Death has removed those in between. Do you get the picture, Clements?"

I whistled softly, and nodded. "Another Mr. A, no doubt."

Magruder winced slightly. All the world knew the scandalous tale of the notorious "Mr. A," which only a few years before the war shook both India and England: yet the central figure of that scandal came to the throne of a proud native state, to receive salutes from many a proud Briton.

"Never mind about that," snapped Magruder. "Ram Lal is dead, or so supposed. Well, Trent's letter of yesterday purported to be from him."

"A letter—from India?" I exclaimed.

"No, no; from here. A letter posted in Los Angeles. A letter saying he was on our trail and that we are destined to perish by the thunderbolts of Indra, whatever that may mean. I fancy it shook Trent up quite a bit, since it threatened his daughter as well. What's more, it mentioned the rest of us."

"Meaning just what?" I demanded. "Oh, the others concerned in the Ram Lal affair?"

"Precisely. As it happens, old Balfour, the prosecutor of Ram Lal, is up at Santa Barbara this very moment spends his winters there and his summers in England, like many a retired pukka sahib. That's three of us in one locality. About the fourth the American teak-buyer whose information led to Ram Lal's

"Listen, old man, you mustn't take this letter seriously," I said. Magruder gave me a hard look. "Trent's dead, isn't he?"

capture, I know nothing at all. The chap was called Chaffee or some such name."

It hit me like a blow. Chaffee! "Are you certain of that name?" I asked unsteadily.

"No, I'm not," rejoined Magruder, pulling at his cigar. "Merely my recollection of it."

Chaffee! Could there be some connection with that poor scarred devil at the Armitage, who had been so long in Tibet? A possibility; yet it seemed far-fetched nonsense. A thousand confused possibilities went dancing through my head. Chaffee's friend—well, he could hardly be Ram Lal, who was Chaffee's enemy. Magruder's story was clear cut and precise; everything else was contradictory and vague.

"Listen, old man, you mustn't take this threatening letter seriously." I turned earnestly to Magruder. "Might have been some sort of joke—"

"Yes?" Magruder gave me a hard, direct look. "Trent's dead, isn't he?"

"Might have been accident. Not even the police are sure about murder." I went on to describe the wound of Sir James, asking if he had any idea of what weapon could have produced it. He shook his head gloomily.

"No. The letter said thunderbolts—the thunderbolts of Indra. He was the Jove or king of the Hindu pantheon, you know; that's all I can say about it. Upon my word, it's all a bit thick! I'm off for home. Here's my card with the address. Have me informed of the funeral arrangements, will you? Count on me for anything needed, of course."

"If you know where to reach Balfour, you might wire him about the funeral."

"Right, when you let me know." Magruder rose. "And do run in on us before long. I'd take you home with me now, but at the moment—well, confound it, I'm upset!"

He was, and no mistake. I gave him my Armitage address and saw him off.

And now—what? Go to the police with this information? Such a course seemed mere folly; the police would laugh at me, for the simple reason that I had nothing definite to offer. That letter had been destroyed, and everything else was hearsay evidence.

Magruder, poor shaken old soul, was a weak reed upon which to lean. And to be honest, I took very little stock in the story he had told me. It was too fantastic, too unreal, to be a logical explanation of Trent's murder—for I felt it to be murder. That thunderbolt business washed it all up for me. Something far more solid and mundane than any thunderbolt had killed Sir James Trent.

Suddenly I recollected Magruder's saying Virginia had also been threatened in the letter. This brought me to life with a startled jolt.

Evidence or not, I had better talk with her about that letter; a warning could do no harm. And for her own sake the police must be informed; she must have some protection until an investigation could be made. Perhaps Trent, too, had dropped some remark that would back up Magruder's story.

All in all, I must see her at once. I rose and went to the desk, thinking to phone her, but the clerk said there was no phone in her cottage. He called a bellman.

"Take Dr. Clements to D-Four," he said. I protested there was no need, that I knew where her cottage was, but the bellman was already on his way, so I followed.

The grounds of the hotel, as I have intimated, were thickly grown with flowers and brush of every description. It was evident that anyone might easily have penetrated the surrounding hedge from the street. If this story about Ram Lal had any truth in it we were dealing with a person prepared to overcome the usual hotel protective measures. All the more reason, I thought, to make sure that Virginia was not molested.

We crossed the grounds and the bellman pointed to a small

cottage almost concealed by enormous clumps of hydrangea bushes on either side its entrance.

"That's the one, sir," he said. "Until last week it was occupied by General—"

I never learned the officer's name. It was cut off by a woman's gasping, incoherent cry—a scream, suddenly and abruptly ended, from the cottage ahead.

Breaking into a run, I came abruptly into full view of the entrance. I had one glimpse of a figure lying on the steps—good God! My warning was too late! In the same eyeflash my gaze went from the woman's figure to that of a man slipping off among the bushes—just a scant glimpse of him, then he was gone.

UPON THE spot, I turned and lunged after him, knowing that the bellman would see to Virginia Trent. The murderer of Sir James had returned to complete his job—and, by the Lord, I had him!

I was into the hydrangeas headlong and through them. He was well ahead of me, running frantically. I saw him to be a slim, dark man, a stranger, who glanced back at me and then legged it the harder. Fear drove him, but a wilder fury impelled me, and I gained rapidly upon him. He ducked in among more bushes, was lost to sight, then I picked him up again as I crashed through. Closer, now—not a dozen feet behind him!

Abruptly he lifted a thin, panting voice, screaming in Hindustani.

"Help me, help me!" It was a desperate cry. "Jaldi jao—quickly!"

I literally hurled myself at him; he evaded. Ahead of us rose a thick, high hedge that enclosed the hotel grounds; the street was outside. The killer tried to break through it, but I was too close upon him. Seeing escape to be impossible, he whirled and wildly struck out at me with something in his hand. Dodging the blow, I went slap into him headfirst.

The impact was terrific, sending us both to the ground and

fetching a gasping squeal from him; he was underneath, and I got him by the throat with both hands. In a frenzy of fury, I banged his head against the ground—I could think of nothing except the figure of Virginia sprawled on those cottage steps.

Suddenly the hedge high above us burst asunder. I looked up, had a fleeting glimpse of two men flinging themselves upon me. This devil had called to them, of course; I was fighting for my life upon the thought, vainly trying to reach my feet.

They had me down—dark men like the first, Hindus. One of them was on top of me. I twisted, got his head pinned inside my left arm, and pumped my right into his kidneys. He screamed frightfully.

"Vajra!" came his voice. "Vajra! Use the thunderbolt—"

That one word flashed everything into my brain. I knew now what had killed Trent, what menaced me.

"Murderers!" I cried, also in Hindustani. "You'll see prison for this—"

In the afternoon sunlight, I caught a glitter above me, a golden glitter—then came a blinding smash, and blackness. Everything was ended.

AMID BLACKNESS, too, I wakened. Painfully, an insistent throbbing in my head. A strange silence filled the blackness.

Gradually proceeding from stuffy chaos to a piqued curiosity, I tried to lift a hand to my head, but had to lift both hands. The wrists were firmly bound together. By the time I was able to finger my scalp, I was coming around very nicely. There was a bump over my ear, nothing worse. No blood at all. I tried to speak, and managed only a hoarse croak. There was a click, and electric lights went on—a perfect blaze, it seemed to my dazed senses.

A face appeared, a figure grew upon me, that of an old Hindu, white-bearded, who stood gazing down at me. An old, calm, kindly face. I might have taken him for a Pathan except for the caste-mark on his forehead—the three tiny horizontal lines devoting a worshiper of Siva, a worship that may involve either flowers or blood.

"So you are awake, Clements sahib!" he said. I blinked amazedly at him and croaked a question.

"You know me? Where am I?"

"In the master's house, sahib. It is lucky that the blow was a glancing one and did not break the skin. I will summon the master."

He was gone before I could summon up any reply in my astonishment. The master? Who the devil was that? And why were my wrists bound with a tight cord? As my eyes became accustomed to the light, I gazed around.

The room was small, but incredibly rich. I lay stretched on a divan close to a flat-topped desk and chair. The walls were entirely hidden by fabulous old Mogul embroideries, each one worth a small fortune. Facing me, against this background, hung a fragment of woven silk in a frame of chased gold studded with precious stones. Why a bit of silk should be thus richly framed, I knew not.

Seeing escape to be impossible, the killer
whirled, struck at me. I went slap into him.

About the walls hung jeweled weapons, all of Indian origin. Upon the desk stood an ancient golden image of Siva, ablaze with diamonds of the antique table cut. Then something else on the desk, beside this image, caught my gaze and gave me a start. Here was the thing that had killed Sir James Trent—this or a similar object! Here was the "thunderbolt" that had stricken me; how simple the explanation!

It was a vajra, one of the cult ritual implements of Hindu worship, representing the thunderbolt. This was probably made of polished bronze; it glittered like gold. Five darts were shown, bound together. That in the center projected beyond the others, which curved in around it. That central point had killed Trent, while the other points merely broke his skin. A thunderbolt indeed, and a deadly one!

Something else appeared closer to me, not six inches from my eyes; loosely hung on a hook protruding from the embroideries, was a Maratha dagger. It had a shagreen or sharkskin sheath glittering with several enormous emeralds—a glorious thing.

Thus, as I looked around, the impression rushed upon me of vast riches, of menace, of peril—and there was the Maratha knife, almost within reach!

My brain was fully awake now. I twisted myself sideways, toward the wall, and my fingers could almost touch the dagger. Another straining effort and they touched it, got it by the handle, grasped it. I let myself relax. The hook pulled out of the wall. The heavy, emerald-studded sheath fell to the floor behind my couch.

The knife itself remained in my hand!

Where I was, the confusion of recent happenings—all this mattered little; escape was the thing! Desperately, I made shift to move the knife and turn it so that it would bear upon the cords binding my wrists. I was clumsy about it. The razor edge of that broad, flat blade touched my arm and parted my skin—then it reached the cords.

Indeed, I felt them give, and give again as a strand parted. Abruptly, to my despair, the knife slipped from my almost useless fingers. It fell between my thigh and the wall behind the couch. It was gone. I could not reach it at all.

IN VAIN I strained. Then, panting and exhausted, I relaxed to wait for new strength. The tingling in my fingers told me the cords were loosened; I could see them partly cut through. Blood from my slit skin welled over one wrist; I inched my sleeve over it.

At this moment the room door, facing me, swung open.

In stepped the dark, handsome man I had seen at the pier and again at the hotel—the man who knew me! I stared at him in stupefied recognition. A glimmer of the incredible truth broke across my brain. He must be the same man whose life I had saved at the Lacpore hospital. Three years ago—just about when Ram Lal had been shot to death. Then this man must be Ram Lal—or was I crazy?

"Well, Clements, I'm glad you're awake," he said. Seating himself in the desk chair, he swung around facing me. "I've kept you tied up, merely as a precaution—hello!" He leaned forward then, looking into my eyes. "What's this? You know me?"

Did he read it in my look—was he a mind reader? He laughed, leaned back in the chair, amused. I lay transfixed, staring, horrified, and afraid.

"Oh, I see! Colonel Magruder came to the Hotel Vista, you had a talk with him—and he told you enough to clear things up, eh? And now you've realized the truth of the situation. I didn't know you were a friend of the Trents. We all make mistakes, don't we?"

He reached out to the desk, took up a cigarette, lighted it.

He was entirely calm, with that curious air of being impervious to emotion. His tone was casual, as though he were discussing the weather. I tried to speak, tried to make some reply, but the words choked in me.

"So you know the truth, or rather, you think you know it," he resumed. "You think I am that dacoit, Ram Lal, of whom

Magruder probably talked. But in fact I am the Rajah of
Sirvath—at least by right of birth."

"They're the same," I blurted. He gave me a slow, curious look
and a shake of the head.

"Not at all, my dear Clements; but the English think they're
the same. Ram Lal was just a dacoit who died in the jungle. As
it happens, since leaving India I have become a very rich man.
Therefore I have power, and the ability to surround myself with
things of art and value. You observe this fragment of silk in
the golden frame? A Sassanid doublet. Silk woven under the
Sassanid dynasty of Persia fifteen hundred years ago; there are
not six such pieces in existence. This one cost me a quarter of a
million, and is worth it."

With an effort, I broke the chains of his hypnotic manner.

"Are you—did you murder Sir James Trent?" I demanded.

"No, I did not," he said coolly. "Clements, you have guessed
the truth. I was your Lacpore patient. When you found me
dying in the streets like a dog, you brought me back to life. That

I thought of Virginia, a crumpled little heap
of garments—and then I had him.

action was destined to reach far into the future—into what is now the present."

He had not killed Trent? He was not Ram Lal? His denials bewildered me, confused me. I did not know what to think, what to believe.

"Then how did I get here—why am I here?" I demanded.

He pressed out his cigarette and turned to me, intently.

"Earlier today I told you that I never forget an injury or a kindness. You saved my life, brought me out of hell, gave me a chance to escape. We belong to different races, but we're both men, and certain things are alike the world over—impulses, reactions, and emotions. Let me tell you the truth. Years ago, when evading the law, I joined the party of dacoits led by this Ram Lal. I was no thief, no murderer, no dacoit. I want you to believe this, Clements. I hold you in respect and liking and gratitude. I belonged to that band, but I was no participant in their crimes."

I almost believed him. His vibrant tones thrilled me with their magic. His steady, luminous eyes fascinated me. I lay staring at him, aware that I was at last hearing the background of this whole affair. The door was opening.

"A rascally teak-buyer, captured and ransomed by Ram Lal, wanted publicity and rewards," he went on. "When that man was a prisoner of the gang, I saved his life. I saw to it that he was ransomed and rescued. Like yourself, he was an American. His name was Chaffee—not Howard the man you helped, but a brother, Gerard Chaffee."

He smiled at my fresh bewilderment.

"This Chaffee later caused my capture. Ram Lal was dead, but he identified me as Ram Lal, after Colonel Magruder captured me. The British thought me a Moscow agent and were frantic to be rid of me. I did not resist arrest, for I did not realize what depths of treachery awaited me. Others were bribed to sustain Chaffee's identification of me. It was a great thing for the government to have captured Ram Lal, you see."

"That sort of thing can't be done," I said. "You have a name. You could prove your identity."

His brows lifted. "The nephew of a rajah? No! I dared not proclaim the fact. My silence was desired; the family bought it with promises of wealth. I did impart my real name to the judge who tried me, Sir James Trent. He called me a liar. The British still ruled India and wanted me to be the notorious dacoit, Ram Lal."

His face darkened. For an instant he was silent. I no longer disbelieved his story; I knew he was telling the exact truth. Everything was coming straight at last.

"I was tried and sent to prison for life—I, under the name Ram Lal. I, who had committed no crime, was doomed, cut off from the world for life. Four men accomplished this thing, Clements. Do you wonder that I came to hate them with all my heart? I had no hope, except in escape. Well, the Japs invaded Bengal and in the tumult of war, I escaped, was badly shot and nearly died—but I am alive, thanks to you."

So it was an escaped criminal whom I had saved in Lacpore.

IT IS impossible to describe the intensity of the man. He remained perfectly cold and calm; but like that black gem in his cravat, he was inwardly alight with crimson fire. This man of stone actually held me spellbound with his blazing force of character. And seeing what was coming, I shrank from the revelation.

"Four men! Chaffee, Gerard Chaffee, went his way, got the rewards offered for Ram Lal, and is today a rich man. Sir James Trent, who refused my plea for justice, went his way. Magruder got a decoration and went his way. Balfour—ah, that pig of a Balfour!" The intonation of his voice deepened. "He, the prosecutor, got money out of it too, and went his way. And now?"

The long, slim fingers of his hand moved spasmodically.

"I am here. I, the Rajah of Sirvath! Those four men are—or were—all in this country. Do you understand? One of them has paid in full. Now I am free, powerful, not striking with unseen hand but giving them full warning. Death is no great punishment, but to them it seems terrible. Trent was the first—"

"And his daughter," I cut in. "You killed her, too. You lied to me."

His head jerked up with a strange dignity.

"No lies. I am sorry she was killed," he said quietly. "And I did not do it."

"You caused it," I snapped at him. "Your revenge may have been justified, I don't know. But when you killed an innocent, lovely girl, you stepped over the mark."

He leaned forward again, as though startled. "So! So that was it! I see why you came straight to them on landing. Clements, look at me, believe me! I swear to you that I meant her no harm. I threatened her in the letter, yes, merely in order to stab Trent more deeply. It was that fool Chandra who got his orders mixed. He killed the one, then went back to kill her. Well, he paid for his mistakes."

Again I found myself believing him, and struggled against it. Agitation had come into his features; then he banished the emotion and became again impassive, cold.

"Those four men who wrecked my life shall die. Human life—bah! You know how little it means in the scheme of things. And you're in no danger from me, I assure you; I owe you a great debt. You can't hurt me. And want you to know the truth about me, the reasons for my acts. About that girl—I am sorry, really sorry, Clements. If only she had not been harmed! Now you have become my enemy, and I regret it."

I did not want to think about Virginia. My incredulous horror had quieted. I spoke at him almost calmly, for now I was facing reality.

"You imagine that these four men deliberately wronged you. They did not. Perhaps Chaffee did, but not the others. They may have been guilty of mistakes—and you seize on that pretext to go into an orgy of murder and whine about your wrecked life!"

"How singular that you, who saved my life, should know any

of those four men!" he said almost musingly. "I did not suspect it. My agents failed me there. But you're in no danger; I owe you my life. Luckily those men of mine, hearing you speak Hindustani, fetched you away with them. I shall set you free."

"You'd better not," I said. Thought of Virginia lying dead on those cottage steps maddened me. "I'll see you hanged for those murders if it's the last thing I ever do!"

He smiled slightly. "Keep your poise, Clements. You'll do no such thing; I'm far beyond your reach. Besides, the police would laugh at your story; they already have the killer of Trent and his daughter."

"What?" I exclaimed, startled.

"Certainly—the man whom you pursued and caught, Chandra. You fractured his skull. My other men left him there. Lying beside him was the bronze vajra that killed Trent and the young woman; thus, the evidence is complete. Further, Chandra is already wanted for a murder near Fresno. I pick my agents with care, you see."

He had me blocked, baffled.

"But you planned it—" I began.

"Come, come, man! You can prove nothing. You have no evidence. You don't know the name I'm using here. You don't know even where you are at this moment, in what city of your charming California this house stands! You're helpless." He paused, thumbed his thin black mustache, and I thought he stifled a sigh. "I shan't harm you. I've sworn to repay your kindness, and my own oaths are sacred things—"

"I want nothing from you," I said hotly. He must have read the hatred in my eyes, for his own gaze narrowed upon me. "For what you've done this day, I'll get you if it takes the rest of my life!"

"Because the girl died—you mean it," he said. "What a pity! Well, it cannot be helped. Even I, who have planned so carefully, make mistakes. For I am careful, my dear Clements—look at Howard Chaffee, whom you treated. He's an American who disappeared many years ago while on an expedition to Tibet. It has cost me long work and much money to get him here safely. Through him I shall strike Gerard Chaffee, the brother who so injured me. Well—enough of this talk."

He rose, picked up a fresh cigarette, lighted it. I had nothing to say. Virginia Trent was dead; it took the heart out of me.

"You'll be given a hypodermic and then sent back unharmed to the Armitage," he said. "Let me warn you in one respect, Clements. You're safe from me; but if you interfere with my agents, you're not safe from them. That's all."

He went out of the room with swift, silent tread, and the door closed.

I lay in an agony of futility and impotent anger. Everything had opened up, and I realized how impregnable was the man—Ram Lal, the only name I knew for him. His words were true. I did not know where this house stood, what name he used. The tremendous virility of him was overpowering. Had it not been for Virginia's murder, I could almost have sympathized with his lust for vengeance. He had been deeply wronged, were his story true. Now he was an inhuman thing, without conscience, a man from another world, a man from hell itself....

The Rajah from Hell!

Abruptly, I became conscious of a life-glow in my fingers and hands. Again I made a spasmodic effort. Those half-cut yet binding cords separated a little more. Another effort—and the cords parted!

My hands were free!

ON THE desk was a telephone. Reach it, learn its number—then I would no longer be impotent! Knowledge would arm me to fight this man, to bring him to justice. I was free! The thought was like a star-rocket in my brain.

With a burst of frantic joy, I raised myself and fumbled for the fallen knife. My fingers found it, closed on it. At this instant the door suddenly creaked and swung open. I sank back as I had been, slid the Maratha knife up my sleeve, lay quiet. Into the room returned Ram Lal; with him was the old Hindu I had first seen here.

"Give me the syringe," said my host.

From the old man he took a hypodermic syringe, needle bared, plunger out, and came to my couch. He leaned over me. I thought of Virginia, a crumpled little heap of garments—and then I had him. Flinging up one hand, I caught him about the throat; the cut wrist left a scarlet smear on his golden skin. With the other hand, I plunged the Maratha knife for the heart, thrusting with all my strength.

The steel slid aside; the point would not enter. He wore some protection—

Other men came running. I fought them blindly, furiously, but uselessly they held me down, Ram Lal leaned over me again and I felt the prick as the needle stabbed home. Then by degrees everything faded away into nothing.

When I wakened, it was to a sunlit room—my own room at the Armitage. The following day, obviously.

Turning my head, I uttered a choked word of incredulity. Sitting beside my bed, reading a newspaper was Virginia Trent. Impossible! I was out of my head....

"Doctor! Come quickly—he's waked up—"

Her voice was real. A man came the hotel physician. Presently, the burst of confused questions ended, I was alone with Virginia again, and the amazing reality was fact indeed. That man Chandra had mistaken the nurse for Virginia Trent and had killed the wrong woman.

Beside me on the bed, perhaps as mute evidence of contempt, lay something that had been left here with me—the Maratha knife, complete with shagreen sheath and emerald studs.

I talked everything over with Virginia, of course. The police? I was no such fool. I wanted no publicity, no silly questions.

"England? I'm not going back there, Hugh," Virginia said quietly. "Father is to be buried tomorrow. I'm staying here. Now that everything is definitely known, I must talk with Magruder, with Balfour—"

"You stay out of this business!" I quickly exclaimed. "It's no work for you! This fellow, like most criminals imagines that he was framed and wronged and handled with cruel injustice; he's out for revenge and is dangerous. You can do nothing, the police can't help us—"

"I'm not thinking of the police," she said and gave me a quick, hard look. "Of Colonel Magruder, first; he'll know what to do. I must talk with him."

"No—not you, but we," I said. "I'll see Magruder; I'll go into this with him full steam. You stay out of it. Your father was my friend and you are more, much more."

Her eyes rested on mine with assent and understanding: then she broke down. After a time, I was alone again. She had gone back to Pasadena. I lay there thinking, thinking, fingering the shagreen haft of the Maratha knife.

Magruder? Yes. There was work to do!

THE DIAMOND DEATH

The story of the second Californian marked for
murder by the vengeful "Rajah from Hell."

TWO DAYS after the funeral of Sir James Trent, I was talking earnestly with his old friend Colonel Magruder. Poor Magruder! For him, the devil was indeed let loose, most literally, but he hated to admit it.

This precise, steely, lantern-jawed old British soldier was merely the shadow of himself. Here in California, fate had caught up with him. I told him the whole truth about Trent's murder, and he mopped his forehead nervously.

"Yes, yes, Doctor Clements. It does seem incredible, unreal! Can you describe the fellow? What is he like?"

"But you should know, Magruder. You're the man who captured him."

He gestured irritably. "That was years ago, Clements, in India. Now we're in California. He was only a half-wild dacoit—I don't remember him. How can one be sure he is the same man? He may be lying."

"Sir James Trent was murdered. That's answer enough."

"And his murderer was found dying."

"The actual killer, yes. I'm talking about the man who sent him, the man who threatened Trent—and who will soon threaten you."

Magruder winced. I was deliberately trying to rouse him, of course, for his own sake; unless he acted, I knew he was a doomed man.

After seven years in the north of India—I had charge of the

Anne caught her breath. "But if you know so much—"

Lacpore hospital since before the war—I had barely landed at home when I was tossed into this ugly puzzle of murder. While in India I had known Magruder and the others concerned. After retiring from the service, Magruder lived in Hollywood; a niece of his from Scotland had won some vantage-post in the movies, and he lived with her. Unreal as my story must have seemed, he was aware of the facts, and knew I spoke the exact truth. I went on speaking, bluntly:

"Your nerves are gone, Magruder; don't blink it. Now, I've

seen and talked with this Hindu who is rightfully Rajah of Sirvath. I don't know his name; I hoped you would. He was not Trent's actual murderer, but instigated the crime. He told me so himself and talked freely. You, he said, are next on his list."

Magruder winced again and scowled at me. I gave him both barrels now.

"This Hindu is a man of education, of wealth and culture. I saved his life while in India, and he remembers it. He claims that four or five men railroaded him, framed him, most unjustly. Trent, he says, was one of those men."

"Absurd!" Magruder shifted uneasily. "During the war, Clements, things had to be done hastily but there was no framing, no injustice. That's the fellow's story, of course. Every scoundrel is an innocent victim, by his own tell. This man was identified as the bandit and put away, that's all."

I got it. Identified—by whom? By Howard Chaffee—perhaps fraudulently. Then the Englishmen acted on that identification. They were not framing anyone. Any blame must attach, not to them, but to the American teak-buyer Chaffee. Yet the victim blamed them all.

It seemed unreal, in this sunny living room that overlooked most of Hollywood. The villa was perched on the high hills framing the movieland city. Magruder, with a touch of his old decisive air, turned to me earnestly.

"I've taken every precaution, Clements. My friend Count Marinao has helped; he is consulting with me right after luncheon, indeed, regarding a brace of watchmen he recommends. My niece is most capable, too. She knows this country and its customs and is advising me. The grounds here are well policed at night—"

"Trent was murdered in broad daylight," I broke in. I knew his thought; that I was an obscure physician without wealth or influence, incapable of coming to grips with our enemy. "I'm helping Virginia Trent run down the murderer of her father; for your own sake, you must pitch in with us," I said. "Four men are menaced. One is dead. The other three must get together. Virginia has gone up to Santa Barbara to see Balfour, who lives there. You don't, apparently, realize your own acute peril."

"Yes, I do," said he, then looked around in obvious relief. He probably resented my insistence and regretted his own hesitation. "Here's Anne now, so let the dashed affair rest for the moment. —Hello, my dear! This is Doctor Clements, of whom I've so often spoken."

ANNE MAGRUDER, more famous under her screen name of Anne Hastings, came forward with a cordial greeting. Sunny-haired, trim, graceful, her lovely features and laughing eyes had rapidly pushed her to the front of her profession. She had plenty on the ball.

"I'm dying to ask you a hundred things about India, Doctor Clements!" she exclaimed as we shook hands. "Uncle, those insurance men are here to see you. I'll take Dr. Clements into the garden and make him talk, while you take out the insurance."

"Better take out plenty, Magruder," I said with grim significance. His Scots refusal to meet the greater issue squarely had angered me. With a grunt at the shot, he left us, and I stepped into the garden with Anne.

No sooner were we alone, than she turned on me in warm anger.

"What made you say that? Don't you know that he's all worked up over nothing?"

"Nothing?" I echoed, frowning at her. "Why, he said he had confided in you! And you must know Sir James Trent was murdered—"

"And his murderer, a Hindu, was found dead," she flashed defiantly. "All this talk about some old feud from India, a man seeking revenge, is sheer moonshine. I've tried to make him realize it. So has Count Marinao who is certainly no fool. Then you along and get him upset and terrified. I don't like it! I shan't permit it!"

This was the second mention of Count Marinao.

"Who is this count?" I asked. "One of your peculiar Hollywood nobility?"

Anger sprang in her eyes and voice. "He's a Brazilian gentleman who owns diamond mines, a very good friend, a man of the highest standing."

I shrugged. This fool girl was actually an enemy; obviously, she had spiked my hopes of getting constructive help from Colonel Magruder. I spoke quietly, bitterly:

"Well, my dear, let me as a professional man give you some unpleasant facts: The man who murdered poor Trent was a mere agent. Behind that murder was a man known as the Rajah of Sirvath. Some years ago, in India, he was identified as a notorious bandit and condemned to penal servitude for life. He believed himself framed unjustly; he himself told me so. He holds four men, all at present here in California, to blame."

Her gaze widened on me. "What? Do you know the man?"

I nodded. "One day in Lacpore I picked up a poor devil on the street, half dead and in delirium. In my hospital I brought him back to life; then one night he disappeared. Here in Los Angeles I met him again, the day of Trent's murder. This man was the Rajah of Sirvath, as I must call him for lack of a better name. He is now wealthy, powerful, bent upon being revenged for his supposed injuries."

She caught her breath. "But if you know so much—"

"Listen, please," I broke in. "Your uncle is one of the four men he blames for his supposed injuries. Another is Chaffee. I think he was an American teak-buyer in India, but I know little about him except that he was a scoundrel. Third is the Honorable Fitzjames Balfour, K.C., who is now in Santa Barbara. Fourth was Sir James Trent, now dead, after receiving full warning from the man who hated him. Our enemy is no skulking killer, but gives fair warning of his deadly intention."

She was clearly impressed by my words.

"Have you informed the police of all this?" she asked.

"I've no evidence. They'd call the yarn fantastic. I don't know what name the man uses or where he lives. He's able, wealthy, driven by a frightful sense of supposed injustice. He's a monster, a killer."

Her lovely features were troubled, irresolute. She eyed me sharply.

"And you? Just what is your interest in this affair?"

"Sir James Trent was my friend. His daughter Virginia is—well, I hope she may be more than a friend. I'm helping her to run down the murderer of her father."

"The actual murderer was found dead."

"Yes. I killed him."

I hoped that the bald shock of this statement would put some sense into her head. I should have known better. After all, she was English, or Scots, and a movie actress to whom the cinema world was everything; she would permit nothing to menace the petty illusions of that little world of hers.

"Oh! Doctor Clements, I think you must be out of your head!" she breathed. "Such things—here in California, in Hollywood—why, they simply can't be as you say! They're not real. You may believe all this nonsense, of course, but I beg you not to frighten poor Uncle any further."

"I have no wish to frighten him," I rejoined curtly. "My entire aim is to save his life, if possible. I'm sorry you think it nonsense."

"I don't know what to think," she said. Then, suddenly beaming, she put her hand out to mine. "But I do feel you're honest about it; you mean well. Perhaps you're too fresh from India and its wonderful scenes—"

"Wonderful fiddlesticks! The world is the same everywhere," I interrupted sharply.

Then I was aware of Colonel Magruder approaching us. There was a change in him. He was more himself, firm with military bearing; evidently something must have happened to cause it. He pressed me to remain for; luncheon, but I refused.

"Thanks, no," I said. "I'm leaving my hotel this afternoon. I've found an apartment, and must get moved into it."

"My boy, this gaudy thing set back Mariano a fat twenty thousand pounds."

"Then come tonight, do!" Anne exclaimed impulsively. "I'm having a party—everyone connected with my end of the studio will be there, and half Hollywood besides; a grand and noisy and gorgeous affair. It'll bore poor Uncle stiff unless you're here to brace him up. Any time after eight. We'll expect you."

I ASSENTED. She departed gayly like the useless and artificial creature she was, a butterfly in a world of men and sense and action. Magruder stroked his gray mustache and eyed with grim intentness.

"Well, what's happened?" I asked bluntly.

He grimaced. "Dash it all, Clements—a chap just telephoned me. Spoke Hindustani. Said he was speaking for the Rajah of Sirvath."

"Hello! Our Rajah from Hell in person?"

"No. An old man, evidently."

I whistled softly and waited. He went on with a snap in his voice. The actual contact with peril had restored him to himself.

"Devilish impudence, I call it! The chap said that the Rajah would pay his debt to me within twenty-four hours, in my own house, among my own people. Then he rang off."

I regarded him gravely.

"Magruder, this means business. Our man warns before he strikes; he warned Trent. What shall you do? Count on my help in any way."

MAGRUDER BECKONED to a man who had followed him from the house. Despite his garb of butler, his military figure betrayed the old soldier. A sturdy, capable man who approached and stood at attention. I liked his craggy resolute features.

"Dr. Clements, this is my old striker, Parr, who knows all about the business," Magruder said. "Parr, that Hindu chap just telephoned me in a threatening way. You'll stay armed, and watch every stranger who arrives. The two men Count Marinao is sending will arrive this afternoon. Watch the house and grounds carefully today and this evening. Check on everyone who comes. Take nobody for granted."

"Very good, sir," Parr said flintily.

"And," I cut in, "your bullets won't hurt our Rajah from Hell! He wears some sort of bullet-proof vest, as I found to my cost."

"That won't save him if he shows up," declared Magruder with a snort. "Upon my word, I hope he does come and give us a chance! Well, why are you frowning?"

"I think we should get in touch with Balfour," I replied. "Virginia Trent went to Santa Barbara to see him. He should make common cause with us—"

"Harrumph!" Magruder snorted again. "We can handle this filthy native without help. Balfour's a pompous ass. Trust Parr to take care of the rascal if he does appear."

With this, he dismissed Parr and took my arm as we walked toward the house. I asked him a question about Count Marinao.

"A splendid chap, Clements. Confidentially, I'm sure he has a romantic interest in my niece; I'm meeting him downtown after luncheon. He's rather formal, pleasantly old-fashioned. I fancy he wants my permission to pay his respects to Anne. You're at the Etruria? I'll stop in there this afternoon."

"I'll be there till about three," I rejoined. "Then I'm moving."

"Right. I'll stop in. I'm delighted that you'll come around tonight. I'd like you to size up Marinao—I'm sure you'll take to him."

"I'll come, yes," I told him. "With a pistol in my pocket."

With this, I took my leave, somewhat irritated. Magruder's contempt of the Rajah and the attitude of his niece disturbed me. Knowing so well the Rajah's implacable hatred and deep guile, I had hoped for a union of all our forces against him. I knew that his agents kept me under surveillance; this was why I had taken an apartment, which insured me more privacy than did the hotel.

True, the Rajah had sworn not to harm me, since I had once saved his life, but he had said frankly that with his agents it was another matter. And if it came to death grips he would forget his oaths. For agents, mere pawns to him, he could get plenty of Hindu workmen from the inland regions about Fresno....

Luncheon past, I sat down and wrote lengthily to Balfour at Santa Barbara. I had known him in India, a rather pompous fellow. With Virginia Trent now there to see him my letter would help to impress him, I meant to join her there soon. I urged Balfour to try and locate the man Howard Chaffee. I knew vaguely that he was now rich and settled somewhere up the cost. We needed to present a united front against this deathly terror.

My letter was barely posted at the hotel desk when in walked Colonel Magruder from the taxicab entrance. He was most cheerful, and noting a perceptible bulge in his coat pocket, I presumed he was armed; but my presumption was incorrect.

"Hello, Clements!" He gave me a firm, quick grip and motioned to a corner of the lobby. "Come over here; I want to show you something. Well, it was precisely as I anticipated. The Count has requested my permission to speak with Anne." He permitted a dry chuckle. "My permission, in this day and age and country! Rather a joke, what?"

"You seem to be hugely delighted over it," I observed, as we settled upon a divan before the huge expanse of windows that overlooked the gardens.

"Frankly, I am, and so I should be." With a sigh of relaxation, Magruder sank down and accepted the cigarette I offered. "An extraordinarily fine chap, this Marinao. And a brilliant lawyer, by the way."

"Yes? Anne told me that he owns diamond mines."

"In his native Brazil, yes. Purely as a matter of form, I've cabled my solicitors to look up his family and so forth. Personally, I'm entirely satisfied about him. What's more to the point, naturally, Anne is satisfied. And this, my boy, speaks more loudly than anything else."

He tapped the bulging pocket, giving me a bright smiling glance.

Abandoning the lady with a rush, I plunged through the crowd. Good Lord! Could it be? I must make sure!

"Must be a bank statement, so to reach into your canny Scots soul," I said.

He laughed. "Something just as good, anyhow. I want you to see it Clements. He asked me to allow him to present it to Anne this evening. I agreed and brought it along with me. To be honest, I wanted to make certain the stones are what they appear to be, as I know nothing of such things."

The cautious old Scot produced from his pocket a magnificent case of scarlet morocco upon which Anne's name was stamped in gold. It was four inches wide, eight in length, and quite thick. Magruder unhooked the two clasps and threw back the lid to display, with obvious pride, a handsome necklace of diamonds mounted in gold and platinum.

They were not ordinary stones, but glorious blazing diamonds astonishing to look upon—the sort of thing that one sees displayed in great jewelers' windows. I poked at them with a finger.

"Are they real?"

"Exactly what I asked myself, Clements. Yes, I stopped in at Brook's and had them examined. My boy this gaudy thing set back Marinao a fat twenty thousand pounds! What a present! It'll take Anne's breath away."

"It takes mine away," I said dryly, "to think of you walking about Los Angeles with that in your pocket."

"OH, PARR'S with me; he's just outside now." Closing the case again, Magruder slipped it back into his pocket. He rose, then paused. "I must run along. By the way, I was telling Marinao that story of yours about the Rajah and so forth. He's inclined to take it gravely, and wants to go into the matter with you tonight."

"I'll be glad," I responded. "Anything that may change your attitude will be well worthwhile. I suppose you're going to give Anne a sneak preview of the necklace, eh?"

He shook his head. "No, I had to promise him I wouldn't. He's keen on giving it himself and all that. I told him bluntly I'd like to make sure it was real, and he seemed amused."

As well he might, I thought.

Outside, Parr joined his master stalking close behind him to the car. The very presence of that bulldog of a man was reassuring. I began to think that the Rajah from Hell might have made a mistake in announcing his intentions so dramatically. Nonetheless I regretted that my original plan to take Magruder to Santa Barbara for an immediate conference with Virginia and Balfour had fallen through. Perhaps, I thought, I might get him away tonight following the party. We could drive up there in two or three hours and return tomorrow. I resolved to work toward this objective.

IT WAS close to eight-thirty that evening when a taxi-cab landed me at the hilltop villa, and none too early. When Magruder said eight o'clock, he had meant just that, and I was the last guest to arrive. I was frankly curious to see what a Hollywood party was like. The precautions surprised me. Before the taxi door opened, my name was checked, and at the entrance stood Parr and another man watching all arrivals.

Once inside, I was in the midst of a throng that filled the place to the doors. Of Magruder, at first, I saw nothing. Here were actors, directors, and every other type of person from the studios. Anne took me in hand, introducing me to a host of people, and upon finding a couple of old Anglo-Indians among the guests, I got on famously. Somewhat to my disappointment, there was nothing wild or rakehelly about the party. It was even sedate.

Everyone seemed to know everyone else. Hors d'oeuvres and a buffet supper were on the program, with drinks in profusion, yet a reasonable sobriety prevailed. Most of these people were doing things, and liquor does not assist mental activity. It was not the outlander's notion of a movie party, but it was vastly interesting. I enjoyed it.

After a time Colonel Magruder appeared, making a way

through the crowd to my side. He was obviously in high good humor, heightened by a cocktail, and greeted me jovially.

"Where's your nabob from Brazil?" I asked. "So far, I haven't seen him."

"He was in the library with me just now," Magruder replied, "looking at the necklace. Said he was taking it to give Anne. I imagine they're somewhere about." He glanced around, and took my arm. "See here, Clements! Some of the crowd, old Indians, are coming to the library for a chat and a quiet drink. We'll shut out all this chatter and noise. You know where the library is? Good. Come there in ten minutes or so, then."

Someone called him, and with a resigned look he left me. For no reason that I could assign, his words lingered in my head: "Said he was taking it to give Anne." They had a faintly sinister import, an odd significance. I frowned over them in vain, and could find no cause for my uneasy feeling.

A director's wife who had once gushed over the Taj Mahal at sunrise fastened herself upon me, and for a few minutes I abandoned myself to intensive gas attacks about India. Then, all of a sudden, I was brought wide awake and alert, with sharply incredulous surmise jerking at me.

Threading his way through the throng and making for the entrance doors, was a man. His face I could not see; but his shoulders and back, the proud set of his head—good Lord! Could it be? Abandoning the lady with a rush, I plunged through the crowd after him. His face—I must make sure! The figure, that carriage, brought the Rajah to mind, but I dared make no mistake with so many foreigners in this throng.

Long before I could catch up with him, my quarry had passed out of the entry. At length I shoved my way through the last groups, got outside, found Parr standing there, and caught his arm.

"Parr! Who was the man who just came out—ah, there he goes!" I caught sight of the figure striding rapidly toward a car that stood in the drive, its engine purring. "That's the one! Who is he?"

"That, sir? Why, that's Count Marinao," responded Parr.

This answer staggered me. For an instant I hesitated, then jumped forward. If this were Marinao, I had every excuse to stop him; I wanted to meet him, anyway. But why was he getting into that car, as though to leave? I advanced into the drive, hurrying; my man was already in the car, a foreign cabriolet.

"Count Marinao!" I called sharply.

I was almost at the car when its door swung open. In the house lights, I saw the face of the man who looked out and smiled at me. I heard the voice of the Rajah from Hell, vibrant as a bronze temple-bell.

"Looking for me, Dr. Clements? Too late, my friend—better take a look at Magruder."

The car door slammed; the engine roared; the car leaped past, nearly knocking me down. Marinao—the Rajah from Hell himself! The car was gone. I looked after it, stupefied by the devilish audacity of the man, realizing too late the ghastly truth.

FROM INSIDE the house shrilled the thin scream of a woman.

A commotion had arisen in there. I turned to the entrance, found Parr gone, heard his voice calling me to enter. It was a job; the crowd was in a milling mass, voices were shrilling madly, and working through was a slow matter. Parr stood at the library door, on guard. When I reached him he motioned in, and admitted me.

A studio physician, one of the guests, was in the library with Anne Magruder.

It was she who had screamed. Now she stood pale and silent, looking on, one hand at her face.

Colonel Magruder was dead.

He sat in his chair at the desk, across which he had collapsed. Almost under his hand, open and empty, was the scarlet morocco case that had held the diamond necklace.

The physician was leaning over the desk, holding Magruder's wrist. He straightened up and seemed about to speak, when I saw a swift pallor sweep across his face. I was barely in time to catch him as he keeled over, senseless.

I spoke sharply. Anne, with bewildered tragedy in her eyes, helped me to get him on the couch at one side. He was breathing hard, but now he relaxed. After a moment he appeared to be all right, and leaving Anne beside him, I turned back to the desk.

Neither of us spoke. I touched Magruder's wrist; his pulse had ceased. He showed no sign of any violence; to all appearance he had succumbed to a heart attack. I knew better. The physician's

I was barely in time to catch the physician as he keeled over, senseless.

collapse had given me a hint, and I could guess the rest. Quickly, I went to the window beside Magruder, opened it wide, then returned to the desk.

A glitter there caught my eye—tiny shards of glass. I moved the hand of Magruder aside. Other glass shards showed, so incredibly thin as almost to crumble at a touch, and a slight vanishing stain on the blotter. Even as I looked, it was gone. I took up an envelope and into it gathered some of the glass fragments.

"He's better now," came Anne's voice.

I looked up. The physician was sitting up, looking around with a bewildered expression.

"It—it's my heart," he murmured. "I've had one or two attacks. They come at the most inconvenient times—never knocked me out before—"

He came to his feet, quite all right once more. Anne introduced us. He shook hands, then nodded at Magruder.

"Heart got him, eh?" he said.

I was about to make hot denial, when I saw the steady gaze of Anne fastened upon me. She made an impulsive gesture, and this checked my words. I read her message, and with a shrug obeyed her eyes.

"YES, SO it would seem," I assented and turned to the door. Already the whole infernal scheme was coming clear to me. The gorgeous scarlet of that morocco case, so unusual in color for a jeweler to use, revealed the diabolic cunning of the crime. At my summons, Parr came into the room.

"Have you called the police?" I demanded.

"Not yet, sir," he replied, eyes on the dead man.

"Then go slow. Find either of the watchmen supplied by Count Marinao and bring 'em here—by force. Colonel Magruder has apparently been the victim of a heart attack. Tell the guests and clear 'em out."

Parr departed. I turned to my confrère.

"Doctor, will you help get rid of the guests? You know them, I don't. Then, if you'll be so kind, return here and take charge of the formalities. The cause of death is evidently quite obvious."

Missing the sarcasm in my tone, he nodded and left the room. I swung around and looked at Anne Magruder, who had missed nothing.

"Well?" I said grimly. "Why did you want me to keep quiet?"

She had pulled herself together. Her gaze was defiant, her voice had a bitter edge when she replied.

"Do you think the police could do anything—now that he's dead?"

"They couldn't save him, true." I looked down at the dead man. "Poor Magruder! To think that the very man you feared was pretending to be a friend, tricking you, a Hindu pretending to be a Brazilian! And I unmasked him too late."

My words shook her out of her calm and brought a rush of color into her face.

"Dr. Clements! What do you mean by that?"

"Precisely what I say. I saw the Rajah of Sirvath leaving the house. I followed him. He jumped into a waiting car, laughed at me, and sped away. He was your friend Count Mariano, young woman!"

"Count Marinao—oh, it's fantastic, impossible!" she cried.

"Did Marinao give you the diamond necklace that was in the scarlet case there?"

"Diamond necklace—of course he didn't! I never saw that case before."

Her name was on the top of the case; it might have proved my story, but her shocked incredulity, her actual hostility, silenced me.

Parr came into the room, alone.

"Those two men, sir," he reported. "Not here. Gone."

I turned again to the girl.

"Your uncle has been murdered," I said. "Do you want to call in the police?"

She stiffened; her eyes hardened on me.

"There's not one single thing to indicate murder," she replied steadily. "Your mania is unjustified. Certainly I shall not summon the police."

At this, I perceived the truth; and it sickened me.

"A Hollywood murder story splashed over the newspapers would hurt; you can't take it, eh?" At the scorn in my voice she winced, but her eyes remained hard, inflexible. "Well, the choice is yours."

"Yes, it's mine," she said. "He died from heart failure. A doctor says so."

I made no retort, but bowed silently; the matter was closed. After all, she had herself, her career, to think about. Murder publicity might be highly injurious. There was something to be said for her attitude, but it made her shrink to less than nothing in my sight.

"Do you know Marinao's address?" I demanded.

"Of course. The Roosevelt. He's well known. This accusation you make is so utterly preposterous—"

Her voice died away under the look that I gave her. Turning, I walked out of the room, only to be halted abruptly. Parr was clutching at my arm. His face was white, strained, agonized.

"Beg pardon, sir," came his hoarse voice. "I—I heard what was said. If I might offer you a bit of help—"

"So you don't care much for her either, eh?" I observed. "Very well. Do you want to take service with me— until I'm through with this Rajah from Hell?"

"So help me, I do!" he said fervently. I had read his look aright. "Was it him done it, sir?"

"It was," I said. "How soon can you clear out of here?"

"In ten minutes, sir—now that he's gone. Lor' love me, I've served him these fourteen year past—"

"Get your stuff," I said curtly. "And show me where's a telephone. I'll order a taxicab."

The house was emptying rapidly. Parr showed me to a telephone. The guest physician nodded to me as he went back toward

"Beg pardon, sir," came his hoarse voice.
"If I might offer you a bit of help—"

the library and said something about the coroner. I ignored him and picked up the telephone. I was in a cold fury. Like Parr, I wanted nothing more to do with this house or anyone in it.

After summoning a taxicab. I called the hotel and asked for Count Marinao. I was not surprised to learn he had checked out that morning, leaving no forwarding address.

"Has he been stopping long with you?" I demanded.

"Over a month," was the response. "He has gone back to Brazil, and said he would send his address later."

I went outside and walked up and down the drive, waiting for the taxi.

No use calling in the police; all tracks were covered. Marinao had vanished forever. No wonder he had laughed at me! With that golden skin, he could pass for a Latin of any sort. Count Marinao, with a suite at the Roosevelt, had been in no danger of having his real identity disclosed. His imposture was safe.

How Magruder had died, was only too clear. Magruder had brought the necklace home this afternoon, probably putting it on his desk. On arriving tonight, Marinao had joined him in the library; they had looked at the necklace. Then Marinao had pocketed the scarlet case, ostensibly to present the necklace to Anne.

I could picture the two men leaving the library, parting at the door. Magruder was off to find me and his Anglo-Indian friends, inviting us to a private chat; Mariano slipped back to the library and put a duplicate of that scarlet case on the desk.

Magruder, presently returning, saw the scarlet case lying there and was startled by sight of it. He hastily opened it to see whether it still contained the diamonds. It did not; it contained several glittering glass objects that puzzled him. He fingered them, and under his touch they went to pieces. He sank down as the filmy things collapsed, spilling their volatile fluid. He died, as the fumes clutched at his heart. Long moments afterward, enough of that unseen death remained to cause the collapse of another man, though not his death.

Of course, this was all pure conjecture on my part. It could be confirmed only by a microscopic examination of those tiny filmy glass bits, now in my pocket... I should add that this confirmation was later obtained by me personally.

It was Parr who jumped me out of my reflections. He came running, carrying a suitcase and calling me, as the taxicab appeared.

"Something I forgot, sir," he panted. "I happen to know where the Count keeps his ruddy car. A garage it is, in Los Angeles. We were passing there one day, and I saw his chauffeur awashing of the car just inside. Only a glimpse it was, but there ain't no mistaking that car, Dr. Clements."

Hang the police! Here was what we needed—the garage, a direct line on the elusive Brazilian count! Once we could locate him or his chauffeur, we could go to the district attorney and start direct action. So I popped Parr into the taxi, he gave our driver the garage address, and we were off.

"Just a bare chance, but big enough to reach the gallows," I said. "Marinao would never dream that anyone knew about that garage. A big place?"

"Fairish, sir. A public garage," said Parr. "That 'ere machine is a cabriolet and distinctive."

I gave our driver ten dollars and told him to go fast; he did. On the way, I sketched for Parr how his master had been killed, as I surmised. I liked Parr. He was a hard, grim, faithful fellow, and he had brains. He had a pistol in his pocket, too.

"Suppose we fail, and get no line on our man, sir?" he asked.

"Then we'll rent a car and drive to Santa Barbara, to find Miss Trent and Mr. Balfour. Pompous or not, Baltour's a fighter. I know him. You can return here later for Colonel Magruder's funeral."

Questioning Parr more closely, I learned that the two watchmen supplied by Count Marinao were not Hindus but white men. He had spoken once or twice with the chauffeur, and would know him again—he was a Hindu, certainly.

"Well, let's hope the garage clue will lead us somewhere," I said. "But our man is crafty; the car may not be registered in his name. Don't hope for too much."

A FEW moments later we reached the vicinity of Westlake Park, a once elegant residence section of Los Angeles, now sadly gone to seed.

"Around the corner ahead and halfway down the block," Parr directed excitedly.

The garage hove in sight. It was fairly large but by no means a first class place. I had our driver go past and halt at the next corner. There we alighted. I paid the driver to deliver Parr's suitcase at my own apartment, and the taxi departed.

The two of us walked back to the garage. In the doorway a night man was loafing with a pipe. No one else was in sight. While Parr stepped in, I spoke with the watchman, asking about hotels in the vicinity. Presently we walked on.

"No sign of the car there," Parr said.

"Let's wait a bit. If the car comes, grab the chauffeur—no use trying to trail him. Once we get him and learn where to find his master, I'll prefer a murder charge and get him tangled up with the law."

"And if the man won't talk, sir?"

"Get him, and I'll guarantee that he talks!" I said grimly.

Parr chuckled at this.

We put in a solid half-hour, walking about and keeping the garage under strict observation; the side street was totally deserted. Then, quite without warning, a car came abruptly around the far corner, swung down toward the garage, and drew to the curb out in front. The driver descended and went into the office of the garage.

"Cabriolet, sure enough!" An excited breath came from Parr. "That's him, sir, and the car—driver's all alone. He's not putting it up, either; maybe just paying the bill and taking the car away."

As I fell, the chauffeur fired again and the bullet whistled past my ear. Then Parr, from behind me, dropped him with one sure bullet that drove through his brain.

"Come on! The driver's an accessory to murder—we can't let him get away."

We walked down the street opposite the garage, then started across the street diagonally toward the cabriolet.

The chauffeur came from the garage office into the lighted entry. He was a slim, dark man in whipcord. He caught sight of us there in the street. Some intangible warning must have reached him; perhaps he recognized our figures. At any rate he did not try to reach his car, which was closer to us than to him. Turning, he started up the street—fast. It might have been to see if he were followed or not.

We left him in no doubt. I started after him full tilt, and he broke into a shambling run. Parr dropped behind I gained rapidly on my man. We were approaching the corner when I sent a call after him in Hindustani.

"*Raho!* Stop! I want to speak with you."

He halted, under a streetlamp, and swung around. There was a jet of flame, then a pistol-crack. I was knocked off balance, wrenched around, and pitched sidewise. As I fell, he fired again; the bullet whistled past my ear. Then Parr, from behind me, dropped the man with one sure bullet that drove through his brain.

A police radio car, summoned from the garage, was on the scene within five minutes. My hastily framed story of a hold-up waked suspicion, until the two officers examined the dead man; then all suspicion fled.

"So he tried to hold you up, eh?" exclaimed the sergeant in charge. "Mister, you're lucky; we won't bother you to explain how you had a gun handy. We've been lookin' for this bird a long while; got an ugly mug, ain't he?"

"Looking for him?" I echoed.

"Yeah. Tikat Dao is the name; this is him, all right. Killed a dance-hall girl up near Sacramento a couple months ago. Let's call an ambulance for you; then we'll look over his car."

I refused the offer. The bullet had gone through the fleshy part of my thigh, causing a painful but by no means disabling wound that Parr, under my orders, could see to. My whole interest lay in the dead man's car and what clues it might give.

It gave none. A driver's license was made out to James Drew; the car was registered in the same name, at a palpably false address. There was no scrap of other writing in the car or the dead man's pockets—nothing!

Once more I had failed miserably. An hour later, as I packed a bag to head north with Parr, I fancied that I could hear the mocking laughter of the Rajah from Hell. He had left no trace. He had killed Colonel Magruder, at cost of a car and a criminal's life, and was clear of the law. As I was thinking thus, Parr came to me, and put something in my hand.

"I didn't say anything about this to the police officers, sir. I found it on the sidewalk beside that man. He must have dropped it."

The object was a plain, unadorned ring of silver, set with a single stone. A glittering black stone, which seemed filled with sharp crimson light. A remarkable gem, when you stop to think of it—like a black diamond with a heart of fire. I could not name the stone, but recollection leaped in me.

Not long ago I had seen a similar stone, larger but of the same kind, in the cravat of the Rajah from Hell. Carefully, I slipped it on my finger.

"Good work, Parr! This may lead to something. Bag packed?"

"All set, sir. The car is waiting."

"Let's go."

Two minutes later we were off—off, to the frightful thing that awaited us in Santa Barbara.

THE DEVIL'S FIRE

*Twice a vengeful Hindu prince has carried
out his threat to murder each of four men he
thought had wronged him. Now this Rajah
from Hell warns his third intended victim.*

DRIVING WITH Parr, I got up to Santa Barbara
from Los Angeles at an early-morning hour. We stopped
at a filling station downtown to gas up, and I sought the telephone. After some difficulty I got the residence of the Honorable Fitzjames Balfour—and a very English butler.

"This is Dr. Hugh Clements," I said, "an old friend of Mr.
Balfour just from India. Is he up and around?"

"Yes indeed, sir," came the reply. "He's always about early. Just
now he's somewhere downtown getting an important letter in
the post."

"The devil! Is Miss Trent there at his house?"

She was, and presently I had her on the phone, much surprised
to hear my voice.

"Yes, I'm here, Virginia," I said. "Parr is with me—Colonel
Magruder's man. Magruder was murdered last night."

Her voice broke like a violin-string at hearing this. First her
father, then Magruder!

"Balfour's next," I said. "Tell me what luck you had with him?"

"Oh, the very best!" she reported. "We were driving down
today to meet with you and Colonel Magruder. He'll do
anything you want, will cooperate in any way you think wise.
He's downtown now, mailing a special-delivery letter to you."

I queried her about the situation. She said to come at once
to the house, and told where it was. Plenty of room she said.
Balfour would be delighted to have us.

"Be there in twenty minutes," I said, and rang off before I could succumb to temptation and send her a kiss over the wire. She might not have liked that.

Balfour's place was no large estate. He had retired from his prosecutor's position in the Indian service just before the war's end, and instead of going home to England, came to California. He got in on the ground floor, just before the real estate boom, and took over a nice but not showy place in the new Santa

"The ring turned red as fire, sir!" Parr cried, staring at me. "You have just heard the voice of the Rajah," I said.

Barbara development north of town. We gained it without trouble—a pleasant hillside house with a few big trees around, small grounds, and the walls of big estates on either side. There was a roomy garage with servants' quarters above.

Virginia Trent welcomed us and took us in to breakfast, Balfour was not back yet. The house was thick with his pompous style—two English servants and so forth; a buffet breakfast, and that sort of thing. Having an unpleasantly fresh and stiff

wound in my thigh, I was not very brisk, but said nothing of it. Parr disappeared, and I was thankful for a few moments alone with Virginia.

"Better save the Magruder story till Balfour gets back," I said. "Your report is the main thing, my dear. If Balfour really means business—"

"Oh, but he does!" she exclaimed eagerly. "He knows where Chaffee lives, and has already written him. He has sent to San Francisco for guards. He'll do anything you think best. Mrs. Balfour is visiting friends in Beverly Hills and won't be back for a week, so there's no interference." She looked out of the window. "He's back now."

Balfour walked in and wrung my hand delightedly. He was ruddy, very fit, gray-topped, inclined to pomposity, quite a human fellow on the whole. I spared him the news about Magruder until he had breakfasted; when he found Parr was with me, he guessed the truth, and it shook him frightfully.

We gathered on his screened veranda with Parr and Virginia Trent.

"This meeting is your idea, Clements," he said. "So take charge. Bad news?"

"Very. Let me begin at the beginning Last week I landed here after seven years at my Lacpore hospital—"

I told how I had been thrown into contact with the Rajah from Hell (he was by right, and called himself, Rajah of Sirvath, but I knew no other name for him) and how he proved to be a man whom I had saved from death in Lacpore. Now he was wealthy handsome most capable; then, he had been destitute, a poor devil of whom I knew nothing.

"He holds me in real gratitude," I went on, "but he's imbued with venomous hatred for four men now in California. You, Balfour; Howard Chaffee, whom I don't know; Sir James Trent and Colonel Magruder—and these last two he has already murdered."

"But why?" puffed Balfour. "Why, in God's name?"

"Because you people picked him up as a notorious dacoit or bandit, and sentenced him to life imprisonment. He believes you framed him; he thinks you were unjust—"

"Look here, that's all poppycock," Balfour broke in. "Mere eyewash, Clements! I recall the case perfectly. Government was very grateful to us. You can't accuse us."

"I'm not; I'm telling you his warped beliefs. He was in Russia for a time and no doubt absorbed an anti-English bias. He escaped, you see, during the time of turmoil when the Japs were invading Bengal. He thinks himself a victim of injustice."

I went on to describe the murders of Colonel Magruder and Sir James Trent; it was tough on Virginia and Parr, but necessary. We had no evidence on which to convict the Rajah of the murders. Last night his chauffeur had fired on us, wounding me slightly, and Parr had killed him. I held out my hand.

"There's the proof. Parr found that silver ring beside the man's body."

I TOOK off the ring; everyone examined it. Plain silver, set with a black stone in whose heart burned a red flame—a stone unknown to any of us. I put it on my hand again.

"The Rajah wears a similar stone; therefore I fancy this ring has some connection with him and may serve us," I said. "Now, Balfour, you have all the facts. My idea is that we should combine against this terror. If Magruder had listened to me and had come here yesterday, he'd still be alive. What d'ye think, Balfour?"

"I think you're right," he said. "I've written this Chaffee—he lives in San Francisco. We'll hear from him. He was the one who identified our friend as the dacoit, by the way."

"And you were the King's Counsel who prosecuted him," I said. "Trent was the judge who sentenced him, and so forth. He believes that you fellows framed him unjustly in India—and now he's being tough on you. He murdered Trent, who was my friend and I'm in the business to prove it and get him his just deserts. He knows it, and mind you, won't hurt me; but his men will, quick enough. It's an ironic situation."

We discussed things. My idea was that Balfour would get a warning—the Rajah always gave warning before striking—before long; and that we should get in touch with Chaffee and make every effort to find the Rajah and put him behind the bars. So far, we did not even know what name he used, or where he was.

"Right," said Balfour. "Chaffee should get my letter today. I told him to telephone me instantly he got it; we'll hear from him. How about pulling in the police, what?"

THIS WAS argued and negatived, until we had some actual evidence. During the discussion I got out a cigarette and reached for an electric lighter that stood on the table. As I lit the cigarette, I was aware of a sensation, not painful, but annoying, in my finger. I looked at it. An exclamation escaped me.

The formerly black stone in the silver ring was now flaming red, as though afire! Yet it was not hot, barely warm enough to be felt.

I stared at it, still holding the lighter. So did the others. Virginia started to speak, then was silenced by another voice, faint but distinct:

"—*nothing more at present,*" it said. And it was not speaking English, but Hindustani! *"Look for orders at noon and at midnight. Ghopal Singh or I will speak each time. I shall be in Santa Barbara only a few days. I want everyone to be alert and ready. That is all."*

The voice ceased. Also, the fiery glow died out of the stone in my ring, which again became black and glittering, with just a spark in its depths. When I put down the lighter and cord, the spark lessened.

Everyone, even Virginia, recognized the Hindustani if not the words. All were staring blankly around in search of the speaker. Except for us, the veranda was empty. I was the only one to recognize those tones; it shocked me stiff.

"What a singular vibrant voice!" exclaimed Virginia. "Who was speaking?"

I stood transfixed as he said swiftly: "I want you to pull out of this Balfour thing.... It would grieve me if accidents happened."

"Dash it, that's what I'd like to know!" broke out Balfour. "Hindustani! Some trick of yours, Clements?"

I tried to speak and could not.

"The ring turned red as fire, sir!" Parr cried, staring at me.

I stirred, came alive, found words.

"You have just heard the voice of the man we were discussing," I said slowly, "the Rajah from Hell. Look—it's just past ten o'clock! I picked up this lighter, touching the wire. The ring turned red. It didn't burn, just turned red, blazing red. Touching that wire caused the contact, caused the supersonic waves to take hold, caused us to hear the speaker—some sort of electronics, you see! This ring belonged to the Rajah's man who was killed last night—"

They all began to talk at once. Balfour pooh-poohed the notion, then became silent as I translated the words we had heard. He got a shock, also; evidently the Rajah was here in Santa Barbara. Presently I roused myself and spoke.

"Let's accept what we all heard. Electronics—why not? We know the human body is an antenna, a radio aerial. We don't know the half of what electronic developments arose from the war, here or in Russia. Our man was a refugee in that country, for a time. It's far easier to believe than to disbelieve; that he's an electronic wizard is a fact."

"By your theory," Balfour said, "that stone is a sort of speaker by which he's in touch with his bally agents."

"That's my notion." I handed him the ring. "Test it at noon, twelve o'clock. Touch a wire somewhere, get his broadcast. If it's true, then we, as well as his own men, will be in touch with him."

An electrifying thought; it brought us all up in sharp surmise. Ghopal Singh—as Parr exclaimed, that was not a Hindu name. Sounded like a Sikh. There might be a clue!

Balfour started up.

"I know the police chief here, slightly. I'll run downtown now and get him after information on this Ghopal Singh—won't need to lay any charge. The fellow may have a record, y'know. I'll be back by noon to test the ring. Care to go, Clements?"

I did not. My wound, slight as it was, bothered me when in a car, so Balfour took Parr with him, for company, and Virginia remained with me.

This affair of the ring, while it might afford us a slight lead, rather hit us all under the belt. It indicated the diabolic craft and ingenuity of the enemy. It showed that he was in command of weapons far beyond our knowledge. To be blunt, it terrified us—it did me, at least. The fire in that stone which was not fire at all was frightening.

I bathed quickly, shaved, and rejoined Virginia, feeling much more myself. We went into Balfour's library, where his telephone was located, with the possible call from Chaffee in mind. He had a remarkable lot of Anglo-Indian directories of all sorts and I examined these with quick interest that kindled when I came upon a volume devoted to the Indian peerage and royal houses.

Seizing on this, we examined it together, found the royal Rajput house of Sirvath listed in great detail, and in breathless excitement conned the entries. The present ruler was a brother of the previous rajah, whose only heir had been a son, a young man now dead. He had died during the war, and his name had been Lajpat Rai.

"That's the man," said Virginia. "No one else answers, Hugh."

"So what?" I said. "Our man claims to be the rightful Rajah of Sirvath. Now we have his name—Lajpat Rai. He may not use it, but that's his name, and we have it. Beyond doubt he has papers to prove some other identity, by which he entered the country. Now we put the Immigration people on him, and spike his guns!"

"Grand!" she said. "How are you going to find him to do it?"

This was a facer—it was quite impossible, so far as I could see. However, I felt we had made a step forward, a definite step. His prison conviction under the identity of another man, a bandit, had ruined our man's pretensions to the throne of

Sirvath; this was one reason for his actuating hatred of Balfour and the others. Lajpat Rai was dead—but our Rajah from Hell had been Lajpat Rai.

We were still discussing this discovery when Balfour came back with Parr, and we found it was getting close to noon. Our host was radiant.

"Jolly good work!" exclaimed Balfour, upon hearing our report. "I've done very well, too—excellently, in fact! It was an inspiration to go to the police. They have complete data on this Ghopal Singh. He's a Sikh, right enough; was a worker in the hot district south of Stockton, and is badly wanted for robbery and attempted murder up there last year. If he's in town, they'll dig him out, be sure of that—and his master with him. This Ghopal was a Communist, as well."

"That's no crime," I said. "Andrei Gromyko is one too, and

"If you're on a spot," said the guard,
"there's no sense in wasting time."

lives in a grand estate on Long Island and is popular in Washington."

Balfour winked. "All right, my lad. Wait and see. Getting just on to noon—so we'll try this ring of yours, what?" He reached out and took hold of a lamp cord. "Any wire will do, I suppose. One minute before twelve, by my time."

He stood there, his puffy red face looking rather foolish, but his eyes were intent and combative, his mouth had an ugly set; he could be a nasty customer, I thought, especially when browbeating some poor devil of an Indian radical—a "filthy native," in his estimation.

" L O O K   A T it!" broke from Parr. "The ring! The devil's fire!"

Balfour held up his hand; the black stone of the ring was fiery crimson.

"Twelve o'clock," said none of us. *"No further orders today, my friends."* The Rajah's voice, speaking in Hindustani. Then he switched instantly to English.

"Good day, Dr. Clements. Good day, Mr. Balfour. I trust you are making use of that ring you obtained last night? Make the most of it, I admonish you. A message is on the way to you now. That is all."

The words died out; the ring became black again. I saw Parr looking at me and nodding. Balfour had purpled with anger. Virginia sat tense and white.

"He gives us credit for more ingenuity than we possess," I observed lightly. "He's not certain we've found the secret of the ring; apparently he has sent you some warning, Balfour. You can still clear out of here."

"Be damned if I'll run from him!" snapped Balfour. "Those watchmen haven't come? No word from Chaffee? Huh! I'll stay right here, and if he tries any tricks I'll give him what for! Upon my word—the insufferable impudence of him!"

H E   R E V E R T E D to the practical. The police had been trying out a new radio trick—electronic plates fastened to the walls of a room, and radio reception audible between the plates, nowhere else. Something like that might explain the black stone, on whose properties we had accidentally stumbled. I shrugged; anything was possible.

The butler announced luncheon. Almost at the same moment Balfour was called to the telephone, he rejoined us with a sparkle in his eye.

"That was Howard Chaffee," he announced. "He's driving down from San Francisco. Said he'd get here some time this evening. He has important information on our man. Said he saw in the papers about Sir James Trent's death, and had been at work on the case. Expects a Government man named *Aguilar* to meet him here tonight. Looks definite, what?"

"Pleasantly so," I assented cheerfully. "I knew if we got our heads together we'd get results. Aguilar sounds Spanish."

"Half this town is Spanish, or Mexican, or pretends to be," sniffed Balfour. "They capitalize on it for tourists. Ha! Now I feel better. We can fight back. Chaffee sounded as though he meant business."

I did not mention that, from the little I knew of him, Chaffee seemed to be an arrant scoundrel. I was by no means particular.

We all relaxed under this cheerful intimation, and the meal became almost merry. The coffee had just arrived when a car drove in, and there were Balfour's three guards. We interviewed them—hard-eyed, capable men who obviously knew their business. Balfour told them his life had been threatened, and they, with Parr, were to guard the place.

"I shan't stir from it," he said. "I'll remain here."

"Okay," said one of the three. "That's the ticket, sir. Now let's see the servants and look over the place. We'll answer for your safety if you don't leave the premises. If any visitors are expected, we want to know about 'em."

They went off with Parr, and Balfour beamed at us, and returned the silver ring to me.

"I fancy we have that devil blocked now, eh? What are you

two going to do for the afternoon? You said you wanted to see the town, Virginia."

She assented. "I've always heard about it and have never seen it. But—"

"Then we'll do it," I broke in. "Everything's safe here. We'll see the place, do any errands for our host, maybe take in a movie, and get back for dinner and a big evening with Howard Chaffee."

So, half an hour later, Virginia and I got away for town....

Looking back now at those happenings in Balfour's house, it is easy to realize what childish fools we all were, and I make no exception of myself. At the moment we seemed pretty smart covering every avenue of possible danger and of approach by the Rajah from Hell, as we thought. Yet we were the veriest bungling amateurs, neglecting the most simple precautions. Aware of his deadly rapidity of action, we were hypnotized by it, and absolutely forgot the possibility that he might have made slow and careful preparation toward gaining his ends. I had previously guessed that I was watched in all I did by his agents, and paid small importance to it; I was as much to blame as anyone.

For an hour or so I drove about with Virginia, even taking a look at the vast estates in the southern suburb of Montecito. Then we came back into town, parked the car, and she did some shopping on Main Street. Fascinated by the luxury shops, she vetoed any movie, and we wandered rather expensively about the place, until I was loaded with her packages.

We were in a drugstore buying toiletries when she suddenly turned to me.

"Hugh, will you telephone Mr. Balfour? He said to get some Kleenex if I saw any, because he had run out and did not know where to find it. They have a big stock here. Ask if he wants the white or colored, and how much to get."

There was a phone booth in sight, so I went to it and called Balfour's house. The butler responded; I gave my name, and Balfour came to the phone. I put Virginia's question to him.

"Oh, get three or four packages, any color," he replied. "And—Clements!"

"Yes?"

"I had a telegram half an hour ago, sent from Los Angeles." His voice was quite steady. "It was unsigned, but said something would occur within two days."

"Oh! Sirvath?"

"Obviously. I'm trying to get it traced. Won't do much good, I fear."

I hung up thoughtfully. So he had received his warning. The time limit meant nothing. Lajpat Rai, to give him his true name, might strike at any time. Better not say anything to Virginia about this, I thought, as I pushed open the booth door.

"Ah, Clements! I'd like a word with you—just a word."

I stood immobile, transfixed. There was Virginia, across the store—and here within a foot, smiling at me coolly, stood the Rajah from Hell! Hat pulled over his darkly luminous eyes, he wore natty flannels and looked quite at his ease.

"Glad you found Miss Trent unhurt and well," he said swiftly, as though we were old friends. "I want to emphasize my kindly feelings toward you, Dr. Clements, by asking you to pull out of this Balfour thing—you and her both. It would grieve me if accidents happened."

"Greive you?" I repeated. "You and your cheap tricks—see here, you'll get badly bitten if you keep up this deviltry of yours!"

"As though you or your friends could harm me, or even find me!" he said. "Sorry you're stubborn about it, but I must admit the reason is charming. Well, I warn you: clear out before evening comes—for her sake. I can't be answerable otherwise."

With a nod he turned away; Virginia was coming toward us. My child outburst had been weak, pitiful. There was nothing I could do—no use in making a scene.

"Lajpat Rai!" I exclaimed. He looked back at me, pausing. "What stone is in that silver ring?"

His white teeth showed in a faint grin.

The only heir had been a son, Lajpat Rai. "That's the man," said Virginia. "No one else answers, Hugh."

"An uranium compound, of course! So long."

I WATCHED him out the side door, helpless, unable to think or move. Virginia came to me, smiling.

"Who's your handsome friend— Oh, what's the matter?"

"Everything," I said. "That was the Rajah from Hell—and he answered to the name of Lajpat Rai—here, come along to the soda fountain; we can talk there."

We got a little table, sat down, gave our order; and I told Virginia what Balfour had said, too—no use trying to hold anything back. The drinks came. Virginia was as white as a sheet, but otherwise never turned a hair.

"There was nothing you could do," she said quietly. "Nothing I could have done either, except to lose my head. Glad I didn't know who he was. I'll know him next time."

"His warnings are to be respected and this one was well meant. Think you'd better respect it, and leave?"

"No," she replied. "I can do no good, I know, but I intend to exert every effort to bring him to justice for Father's murder, Hugh. I think we're getting somewhere, too. If one of his men can be caught and made to talk, we'll have him. Balfour has the police after this Ghopal Singh, and Chaffee will give us something important when he comes.... No, I want to wait for developments. Do you blame me?"

I did not, of course. She was the vitally interested party; she was the one to prosecute if Lajpat Rai could be linked with the murder of Sir James Trent. Some attempt on Balfour's life would be made within two days. It seemed safe enough for her to stick around until morning, anyhow. We might even get our hands on the chief devil himself.

So there was no further argument.

Getting to the car, we drove out to Balfour's house, getting there about four o'clock, and called Parr and Balfour into consultation. They heard my report of the meeting, and Balfour urged Virginia to accept the warning and leave. She refused flatly.

"Wait till morning, anyhow," she concluded. "I must hear what Chaffee has to tell us, you know."

"All right, then." Balfour shrugged and assented. "So he says the black stone is uranium? Bosh!... Where's the bally thing now, Clements?"

"Lying on my dresser. Want to give Chaffee a demonstration at midnight?"

"We might," he said. "Hello— What's this, now?"

"This" proved to be one of the three guards, asking for a hearing.

"We've been doing a little checking up, Mr. Balfour," he said. "Your phone wires come to the garage first, then to the house. Why?"

"Eh? How the devil would I know?" said Balfour. "Ask the telephone people."

"Well, it'd be a cinch for anyone living in those upstairs garage rooms to tap your wires. All that's needed is a magneto, or a magnet wrapped magneto style. Who stays up there? The two menservants and the cook, I understand."

"Correct," said Balfour. "Both men have been with me for ten years or more. The cook, Mrs. Brown, was employed by my wife three months ago. Local woman. Steady, reliable and a good cook. There's a phone in the garage, by the way."

The guard grinned. "That answers my first question, then. Suppose Mrs. Brown was a spy and reporting all that was said on your phone here?"

We looked at one another. "Well, we'd be in the soup," said Balfour. "I say! I can telephone Mrs. Balfour in Beverly Hills and get this woman's references, and you can look her up in the morning, eh?"

"I'd say do it now," replied the guard, "and one of us can look her up tonight. If you're on a spot, there's no sense in wasting time. We don't want her to listen in and get wise, though; she's in her room now. I'll go chin with her while you're on the wire."

This was good advice; it would have been better a few hours

earlier. Thought of what any such spy might have reported to Lajpat Rai via the garage phone was disturbing. Balfour called long distance; before he got his wife, the guard came back hotfoot. Mrs. Brown had gone, disappeared—gone for a walk half an hour ago, another guard said. It had not been considered worthwhile reporting. She had carried only a leather armbag.

"With the magneto and wire in it," said the guard, and went off to search the woman's room. The search revealed nothing suspicious, but Mrs. Brown did not come back; and this looked bad, but not necessarily suspicious.

There was plenty of food in the house, and Balfour's two menservants threw a meal together without trouble. Just as we were about to sit down, the telephone summoned our host. He rejoined us, rubbing his hands and chuckling.

"I knew it! I knew the blighter would overstep!" Balfour exclaimed. "They've got Ghopal Singh—found him driving a car that's registered in his own name, and he's behind bars now. The chief said I'd better come down this evening when he's questioned. I'll go in an hour or so... Risk? Poppycock! No risk at all."

"There he goes!" yelled one of the guards, and the gun in his hand spat three rapid shots.

Knowing the infernal craft of Lajpat Rai, I was not so sure; however, it was great news, and put us all into an excited dither. At last we had one of the enemy's men in limbo! A start had been made; the Rajah from Hell was not impervious. It put heart into us all. It has often occurred to me, however, that this lucky stroke of ours may have forced Lajpat Rai to change his plans and get into faster motion....

At any rate, we made a merry meal seasoned with facile predictions on what the morrow would bring forth. The coffee was being served when again Balfour was summoned to the phone by a long distance call. Once more he returned joyously, and picked a fat cheroot from the open box on the table before he explained.

"That was Chaffee on the line. He's at Santa Maria, a town just north of here. Had some tire trouble and was delayed. Hopes to be along here in a couple of hours. He says not to open any fight on our man until we've talked with Aguilar—dashed important. By the way, we've heard nothing from the fellow, eh?"

"Did he say what branch of Government service this Aguilar was in?" I demanded.

"Eh? Oh, yes—Immigration Service."

"Then we may have our man nailed. He probably, almost certainly, entered the country under a false name, and with false papers, and Aguilar is laying for him. Lucky thing Chaffee got into this with us."

"Still, we must catch the wolf," said Virginia Trent, "before we can skin him."

Balfour chuckled over his cheroot but there was an unhappy truth in her words. Laying hands on the Rajah from Hell would not be easy.

Our host, with activity at hand, became a careful general. He meant to be back from police headquarters before Chaffee arrived. He sent Parr to get out his car and to drive him downtown, and called in the three guards.

"No trouble likely tonight," he said "and I'll have a radio car sent to prowl on this road; but keep a sharp eye out just the same. Admit nobody except a man named Aguilar, and another named Chaffee; each will be driving. As soon as I return from downtown Parr will join you, and you'd best form watches to break up the night. That's all."

"What if anyone else shows up?" asked one. "Strangers?"

"Detain them," Balfour directed. "That's what you're here for."

The forces scattered; the car honked; Balfour bade us a cheery farewell and departed with Parr at the wheel. The evening was pitch dark.

I took a look at things outside, and did not envy the guards their job though they were armed and had flashlights. Balfour had one floodlight that would illumine the garage front; he should have had a dozen to cover the whole house and its approaches. Still, two men should be able to guard the place.

HALF AN hour passed. Virginia, at the piano, was playing softly. I finished a cigar and went upstairs. The slight flesh-wound in my thigh was burning a bit, and I decided to put on a fresh dressing. I switched on the lights in my bedroom, and while getting the gauze and adhesive tape, noticed the silver ring with the black stone lying on my dresser. Better take it down-stairs when I went, was my thought; Chaffee would want to have a look at it. We might even test it out at midnight.

My room was at the corner of the house overlooking the drive and the approach to the garage. It was warm weather and the windows wore open. I mention all these details, not because of the importance, but to counter the allegations that have in made regarding the luck of Lajpat Rai. I do not believe it was luck. I am not so sure there is any such thing as luck, even. I do know that the man went to amazing care, and was swift to take advantage of conditions as they were—and this, for some people, means luck.

I could hear the piano faintly. To change the dressing on my hurt was no great job. I removed my trousers, took off the bandage Parr had applied, and went to the window. I had heard a car drive up, saw a flashlight beam stabbing about down below, and heard voices.

"Who is it?" I demanded. "Is that Mr. Balfour back?"

"It's a Mr. Aguilar looking for him." replied one of the guards. Aguilar! So the Government man was here!

"Good," I rejoined. "I'll be down in five minutes. Bring him in."

They never had a chance to bring him in.

I went into the adjoining bathroom to get some iodine, found mercurochrome instead, and carefully dabbed it on the torn flesh; to use that stuff requires attention, because it spills and stains. On top of it I put the cotton, gauze and strips of tape, well fastening the dressing. The whole thing had not taken more than three minutes, if that. I looked approvingly at the result, caught a slight sound, and looked up.

Across the bedroom, the top of my dresser was gushing flame.

I was spellbound by the incredible sight. Flames were rolling and breaking in a wave; and the wave came from that silver ring. It was like a blowtorch, only a hundred times worse. The window curtains had already caught, and fire was bursting up the old-fashioned wooden Venetian blinds. I heard a yell of alarm from outside.

Then I was darting for my trousers. I yanked them on, got bath towels and went to the flames. It was like fighting blazing gasoline; the towels whipped the flames all over the place and started a dozen more fires and the damned ring gushed forth fire until the towel knocked it aside and knocked it under the bed. Then the flames really took hold of things.

Chemical of some sort, naturally we never learned whether some form of radiant energy started the thing, or whether it was spontaneous. The room was a blazing furnace when at length I gave up the useless effort and staggered out into the hall, slamming the door behind me. Virginia was calling frantically at the foot of the stairs; men were shouting outside.

"Get out of the place!" I called to her. "Phone for the fire department!"

Panic had seized me, I admit. Still I got downstairs and to the phone, and sent the alarm before she could do so. Balfour's two servants and the guards were already at my room, and opening it up merely spread the blaze. I got Virginia outside, and got my rented car out of the garage. It was the only thing saved.

Naturally, everything else had been crowded out of my head—Aguilar's arrival and the rest. I was taking the car down the road a bit when Balfour's car roared up past me on its return. The whole corner of the house was ablaze now, and the ruddy glare showed me the faces of Parr and Balfour very clearly.

I STOPPED the car as quickly as possible and hastened back to the fire. Little time had passed, rapidly as the blaze had gained. Balfour was out of his car, running to Virginia and the guards, who stood out in the road, well away from the heat. The two menservants had rigged a hose and were dousing the garage roof, to which the flames were nearly reaching. Everything at this side of the house was in a full glare of light. As I approached, I caught sight of another car standing just past the house—that in which Aguilar had arrived. Parr joined me, shouting questions above the roar and crackle of the flames, and we hurried on to the group.

I caught one of the guards by the arm. "Where's that man Aguilar?"

"Gosh, I dunno!" he said, staring around. "He was here a minute ago—back out of the heat somewhere, I guess."

A distant siren, just then, told of coming help. Balfour strode out from us, shouting something at his two servant. I was watching the flames gush out through the house-wall, and thinking how fantastic and improbable must be my story of the fire's origin. We had all forgotten any thought of danger to Balfour.

Then it happened. From the road edge I saw a tiny spurt of reddish flame; the crack of a shot pierced through the flame-crackle. Balfour threw out his arms and pitched forward in the glare of light.

"There he goes!" yelled one of the guards. I saw a running figure in light gray go darting toward the car up the road. The guard had seen it first, and the gun in his hand spat three rapid shots. The figure fell, rolled over, then was up and in the car. Another guard beside me yelled:

"That's him! That's Aguilar! *Get* him!"

But nobody could get him. A driver must have been waiting with the engine going; the car slipped away and leaped into the darkness and was gone. Aguilar—Lajpat Rai had come giving Aguilar's name, had done his work, had been hit—and was gone. But he had been hit! One of those pursuing bullets had reached him!

Not that this did any good. Just as the fire chief arrived with siren screaming, we dragged Balfour out of the heat, and found him dead, shot through the head.

Firemen arrived, police arrived; water streams blasted into the house and saved half of it, and the garage, from the flames; but Balfour was dead, murdered. Our efforts had accomplished nothing—except, perhaps, to drive Lajpat Rai into this desperately clumsy murder that could not be disguised as being anything else. He must have planned something far more refined and clever. Certainly his get-away was perfect.

Hundreds of cars and a tumultuous crowd poured on the scene. Parr came through it to where Virginia and I were talking with the police chief. He led another man—a slight, inconspicuous little man.

"Here's Aguilar, Dr. Clements," he said. "The real one."

A quiet, small man, saying almost nothing. But he went down to police headquarters with us and sat in on the investigation. Chaffee showed up later, upon his arrival. He was not so old as the others, being in his early fifties; a spry, leathery-faced, hard-eyed man, also with the ability to keep silent, and a bad egg in spite of his money. He was in time to hear everything and put into dry blunt words what the police chief would not say.

"It's a bust, Dr. Clements," he murmured to me. "The beggar's made a bloody fool of us again, and we're damned well bilked."

AND THAT was precisely the case. The single fact on record was that Balfour had been shot; by whom, none could say. Nobody had identified the murderer. In fact, the coroner next morning got a verdict from his jury of person or persons unknown. The hunt went out for the person we described as Lajpat Rai—and that was the end of it, practically.

"Not quite, of course," Aguilar said that afternoon. He, Parr, Chaffee, Virginia and I were in consultation. "He entered the country with false papers, under a false name. That much remains fact, and it sells me chips to sit into the game. That's a crime. We can't pin Balfour's death on him, maybe. We can't pin Colonel Magruder's death on him, maybe. But he's an accessory to the murder of Sir James Trent; do you want to make that charge, Miss Trent?"

"I certainly do," replied Virginia.

I nodded to her.

Howard Chaffee, who had done very little talking to now, spoke up.

"I haven't had much chance to gam with you folks, but by all accounts I'm next on the list of this Rajah from Hell, so I'd better take the ball and run with it. I've got a place up at Frisco, no family, lots of room, and I aim to give this guy one hell of a fight when he comes along to monkey with me."

"You'll probably have a respite," I said, "since it's pretty sure he drew a bullet last night and may be laid up temporarily."

Chaffee nodded. He was a cool, level-headed sort, and while disliking him heartily, I felt he was the right man for us.

"Okay, then, if you folks want to join in, come along," he offered. "I can use help, yes. Parr wants to get him because of the killing of his master, Colonel Magruder. Miss Trent has her father's murder in mind. Aguilar has a Government job to handle. You, Dr. Clements, have no direct interest—"

"But I have," I said, and met Virginia's eyes for an instant. "Sir James was my friend, and I'm assisting his daughter. Also, I'm the only one of you all who knows the man and can identify him, so that lets me in. Further, I didn't tell the police the truth about how the fire started last night. The truth would be incredible."

Then and there, I gave it to them. Told them about the ring, the black stone, what Lajpat Rai had said concerning it, and what I had seen as the fire's origin.

"Nothing mystical or occult about it," I concluded. "Nothing fuzzy about my brains either. What I saw, I saw, and I can't explain it. Take it for what it's worth."

There was a silence while they eyed me. Then Aguilar spoke in his soft, quiet way, almost apologetically.

"Electronics happens to be a hobby of mine," he said. "During the war I was working with the navy on radar, and the many other electronic devices that were invented. What you've just said, Dr. Clements, is quite credible. I'd say it's clear that this man we're after is an electronics and possibly a radium expert, and therefore dangerous and most interesting in Government eyes. He learned of my expected arrival from the wire-tapping servant and came in my name—impersonating me. I fully intend to wire Washington regarding the issue of a special warrant for his arrest. And for the near future I expect to be located in San Francisco. Do I make myself clear?"

He did, at least to me, for his sidelong glance at Howard Chaffee gave me a hint. He did not entirely like the company he was keeping; nor did I blame him.

"Okay, folks!" Chaffee rose blithely "I'll get back up to Frisco. You have my address, so show up as soon as you're done with the formalities here. We'll set a trap for Lajpat Rai that will settle him for keeps!"

He little dreamed who would be the victim of his trap—nor did we.

HE WHO SETS A TRAP

Four men have been marked for death by the vengeful Hindu who has earned the name of Rajah from Hell. For three of the four have been murdered; and now the fourth is threatened....

JOHN AGUILAR was a quiet, efficient little man in or from the Immigration Service. The day after we got to San Francisco, he sat at lunch with us in our hotel—a small select place far out on California Street. Virginia's English prudery thought it undesirable that we should be at the same hotel; under the circumstances, however, it was necessary, and of course our rooms were on different floors.

"So far," Aguilar said, "I've not received the green light from Washington, but I'm working on the case. Have you seen Howard Chaffee yet?"

Virginia Trent shook her head and gave me a look.

"No. We're going to see him tomorrow. Dr. Clements distrusts him."

"Oh!" Aguilar cocked an eye at me. "We're joining forces to save this man from murder—and yet you don't trust him?"

"Be hanged to saving him!" I said flatly. "Look: Lajpat Rai, the so-called Rajah from Hell, came here from India in order to kill four men who he thought had wronged him during the war. Three of them are now dead, Miss Trent's father among them. I've joined the effort to bring the killer to justice because Sir James Trent was my friend. Also, I know Lajpat Rai personally and in India I saved his life, and he's grateful to me. I don't care a hoot if he kills Chaffee, whom I dislike heartily—in fact, I think him little short of a scoundrel."

"Personally," Aguilar said softly, "I fancy you're right about it."

"Thanks," I said with sarcasm. "You're in it because Lajpat Rai entered this country under an assumed name, with forged papers, and because he's an expert in electronics who has turned his knowledge and aptitude to crime. But evidence—"

"Apparently you have none that will convict him of murder," Aguilar observed; "I have none to convict him of anything else—but I hope to get it. Every scientist in the world is playing with electronics and uranium, these days. Washington holds up my green light, and I'm helpless."

"As regards Chaffee," I said, "I have definite information—but I'm not telling. It may prove damned important."

Virginia eyed me speculatively, and Aguilar chuckled.

"Clements, I like your style," said he. "Talk when ready, not until; that's my motto also. I must warn you two people that Lajpat Rai will have you closely watched."

I nodded. "Understood. But he doesn't regard us as enemies. In fact I'd not be surprised if he called on me for help one of these days."

Aguilar asked for no explanation of this statement, but rose and shook hands.

"I'm off. I know where to find you; you'll hear from me. I'll give you a ring tomorrow night to hear what develops with Chaffee; for the present, I feel like leaving that man alone. So long!"

He departed. I ordered some more tea; I had become an addict to tea during my years in charge of a hospital in northern India.

Virginia was still eying me.

"Come, Hugh! You have some secret about Chaffee. Telling me?"

"My dear, I love you, I hope to marry you, I want to spend the rest of my life with you," I replied. "But my knowledge remains a secret from everyone—except perhaps from Howard Chaffee himself."

She frowned, then the frown dissolved into a smile.

"You'll make an admirable husband, Hugh," she said, not too lightly. "So few of them seem to know how to keep secrets! Mr. Aguilar keeps them too. We didn't learn much from him, did we?"

I smiled. "I planted bait. He'll burn to learn all I know, and will talk when the time comes. Tomorrow night he'll be still more curious. Howard Chaffee was a teak-buyer in India before the war; that's all we know. Yet he now arrives home, long after all the fracas, with a pocket filled with spending money. What I know is more definite; Lajpat Rai told me, so it's just hearsay. I'll prove up on it some day.... Well, it's too bad this is such a public place—I like it, otherwise."

"Too bad it's public? Why?" Virginia's eyes widened.

"The well-known biologic urge tells me to kiss you, but reason says you wouldn't appreciate it here. Let's take a taxicab and go

"Arrgh! Story's a lie!" snarled Chaffee. "I knew him.
My own brother was killed by those dacoits."

down to Chinatown; then people will think we're honeymoon-
ers and won't care."

"Oh! I've never seen Chinatown," she said demurely. "And
I'd love to."

For a young woman who had spent most of her life in India,
Virginia Trent had a surprising eagerness about Grant Street
and its Oriental shops. We bought some rather good tea and a
few knickknacks. I tried to lure her into looking at engagement
rings, but she balked at spending so much money; evidently I
would have to select one on my own.

WE SPENT a charming afternoon and quite forgot Lajpat
Rai. I was not worried about him particularly, because a week
ago in Santa Barbara he had apparently stopped a bullet, after
Balfour was killed, and I thought he might be out of the game
temporarily.... Wishful thinking, of course.

On the following afternoon Chaffee came for us in a swanky
big car. He asked where Parr was. Parr, who had been Colonel
Magruder's man, had attached himself to me after the murder
of his master.

"He was called to Los Angeles, on some affair of the estate,"
I said. "He'll be here in a few days. So there are just the two of
us at the moment."

Chaffee, leathery, hard-eyed, slangy, tucked us into his car.
He was in his early fifties, I judged, and hard as nails. He drove
us west to Golden Gate Park, then south to the western flank
of the hills. The seaward side of the city stretched out before us,
and the ocean beyond, bordered by the Esplanade.

"Got a quiet hillside place," he said. "Nice district, all built
up solid; Chinese boy to look after things. The Rajah from Hell
won't crack this nut very easy. Wong can use a gun too."

It was a snug, secure place—a small stucco house and garage,
bordered by stucco walls eight feet high, with a garden behind
and a high iron-spiked fence in front. Inside, the house was up
to date, handsomely furnished, and Chaffee was rightly proud
of it. He had trophies of various kinds from Burma and India,

and displayed them with a childish vanity. He was showing us a book—a Persian manuscript—containing some remarkable Mogul miniatures, which he had found in Nepal.

"A bit o' loot," said he. "All kinds of agents there—Communist, Jap, Chinese, Soviet. This here Lajpat Rai was one. I got this book from his effects. It was me identified him as the famous bandit when we nailed him."

"He claims it was all framed on him, and false," I said.

Chaffee snarled. "Arrgh! That's a lie! I knew him. My own brother Gerard was killed by those dacoits near the Tibet border. He had done well, too, and had made money. Why, he had two teak companies goin—"

Something fell out of the book and slid to the floor; a small slip of paper on which a few words were written. Chaffee picked it up, glanced at it, and his leathery face went white. He hastily pocketed the slip of paper and called Wong, questioning him about any strangers who might have been in the house.

Wong was an alert, cheerful fellow, no longer young, and spoke fluent English. Nobody had been here today, he said; but yesterday a man from the electric-light company had called and checked up on wiring installations.

Chaffee dismissed him and led us out into the garden, which was private and charming. Delicious tea was served with mint and jasmine, and our host spoke of Aguilar.

"He couldn't show up today. Acts sort of huffy, if you ask me—standoff guy. Well, I have some information on Lajpat Rai. I'm willing to throw in the pot, and if Aguilar won't work with us, he can go without. You ready to talk business, Dr. Clements?"

I said yes, and asked if he had hired any guards.

Chaffee sniffed impatiently.

"No. When Parr comes, he and Wong can act. The fewer people around, the better. Do you think Lajpat Rai is here in town now?"

I shrugged. "You know as much about him as I do."

"Well, step inside to my den, while I get that data on him. Excuse us a minute, Miss Trent; be right back."

We went into the house, to a pleasant den overlooking the garden. Here Chaffee produced some regal cheroots, and taking one, I ventured a question.

"Pardon the personal angle—there's a reason. Did you inherit a good deal of money from your brother who died in Tibet?"

"Aye. Everything. A goodish lot." Chaffee turned, his sharp eyes boring into me. "Who told you that?"

"Lajpat Rai, the Rajah from Hell. He also said your brother was not dead but alive, that he had rescued him and was keeping him safe. I thought I'd better warn you."

The man stood stock-still. After a minute he took from his pocket the bit of paper that had fallen from the book and handed it to me, without a word. I looked at the writing:

"I'll drop in to see you one of these days. —Gerard."

"That's his fist," said Chaffee. "How did it get in that book? Electric man, yesterday, slipped it in. Nobody else has been here. That devil Lajpat Rai is at work, all right! Well, thanks for letting me know."

I followed him back outside. We said nothing to Virginia of this byplay, but settled down with our cheroots and Chaffee gave me the information he had gathered. This was that Lajpat Rai had entered the country at San Francisco six months ago, under the name of Hari Lal, a student, and had papers to prove his identity.

"All forged, of course," sniffed Chaffee. "Aguilar can sweat on that, all right. It's his business. Who can prove that the guy is actually Lajpat Rai, though? That man is supposed to be dead back in India—heir to the Rajah of Sirvath."

"You're getting things balled up," I said, and Virginia laughed uneasily. "I want evidence that he was accessory to the murder of Sir James Trent, which he was. He has killed three of the men who allegedly framed him and jailed him in India; you're the fourth. If he's deported, aren't you safe?"

"Until next time, maybe," Chaffee said sulkily. "I want to see him planted. And that's what I want from you—help in locating him. You know him. You tell me where to find him, Clements; that's all. I'll see to the rest; I've got ways and means. But it's got to be soon—inside of two days."

RELATIONS WERE becoming more strained. I liked Chaffee even less. Now, for the first time, I suspected his pose of wanting no one but Parr and Wong there. He was playing a

A well-dressed man overtook me. "Beg pardon,"
he said; "are you Dr. Hugh Clements?"

deep game of some sort. I was glad when Virginia made a move to depart. Chaffee ran out his car, insisting on driving us.

"We don't seem to be getting far with any campaign of precautions," I said to him as he drove over Twin Peaks road and headed downtown.

He chuckled.

"Leave it to me; it's my fight," he replied. "What I want is all the info I can get on this fellow Lajpat Rai. Give me whatever you get. Send Parr to me—he's an honest man. That house of mine will make the prettiest trap you ever saw."

"He who sets a trap," chimed in Virginia, "had better be sure what game he expects to catch in it, Mr. Chaffee."

He chuckled anew at this. "Thanks. I'll bear that in mind, Miss Trent."

He delivered us safely at the hotel, gave me his card and phone number, said we must keep in touch, and drove away. I was glad to see him go.

Finding no mail, I guided Virginia into the tiny cocktail lounge, found a table for safe conversation, secured the proper drinks, and said:

"All right, my charming partner let's have it."

"Have what?"

"Your reaction. While in his den, I gave our associate a hard jolt, but he made no comment. I think he's double-crossing us—that is, holding back. Keeping his boasted ways and means strictly to himself! While in India, he pocketed fat rewards for false testimony, so I'm entirely willing to think him a black-guard."

"My feeling exactly," she agreed in her quiet way. "And I'm sorry we're associated with him, Hugh; I'm sorry you are."

"I'm playing a game of my own," I said. "I expect something to come of it. In another day or two I'll tell you all about it, my dear—so give me the satisfaction of seeing whether my expectations come true, as I think they will."

She laughed softly. "As you like. When does Parr rejoin us?"

"I don't know yet. Chaffee wants his help, seems to trust him."

"For obvious reasons," she said. "Parr was utterly devoted to Colonel Magruder. He wants only one thing—to get the man who murdered him. And being an old soldier, he's absolutely ruthless and will stop at nothing; that's why Chaffee wants him."

I whistled softly. English girls can be smart as whips.

"You're positively clairvoyant at times," I said.

Virginia finished her drink and rose, smiling at me.

"Probably that is why I like you Hugh," she said, and left me to figure whether it was a compliment or not.

Aguilar, as he had promised, gave me a phone call that evening.

"I had a letter from Washington today," he said. "Indefinite: a checkup is being made with atomic bomb people and I'll hear in due course, and so forth. Irritating! Everyone passes the buck and is afraid of decisions. You have any luck with Chaffee?"

"Yes and no," I replied. "Our friend entered the country here at San Francisco six months ago under the name of Hari Lal—papers okay."

"Ho! That's fine—I can check on that, you bet. And that's not his name. But who can prove it?"

"So far, I don't know. But he'll have a hell of job proving it is his name! However, that's your pigeon, not mine. I don't care about seeing him deported, nor does Chaffee. In fact, the latter wears thin on my nerves. Miss Trent and I don't fancy him, and I suspect his intents and purposes."

Aguilar cackled a thin little laugh.

"Excellent man, Clements! So do I, between you and me. I'd advise keeping Miss Trent on the sidelines; I rather think our excellent Chaffee is playing with firecrackers. I'll know more about that in a day or two."

"Oh!" I said. So he knew something. "Which Chaffee?"

"Which Chaffee?" echoed Aguilar, puzzled. "Just what do you mean?"

"Well, I may know more about it in a few days," I said. "When you feel like explaining about your firecrackers, just let me know. Good luck."

I rang off, knowing very well that he would understand perfectly. An amazing little man, this Aguilar; but he had to be reined in sharply, and I meant to do it.

That is, if my expectations came to anything. It was purely a gamble, but in view of what had happened before, I did not mind the risk.

CHAPTER II

THE VERY next day, my expectations bore rich if somewhat perilous fruit. This was extremely lucky, because Chaffee had given me a two-day limit in which to tell him where Lajpat Rai might be found. Not put as an ultimatum, of course; all the same, I felt that anything Mr. Howard Chaffee might say was to be regarded with a serious eye. As Parr had expressed it after their first meeting, the leathery-faced gentleman was a stinger; and very well put, I thought.

The situation was one of almost ludicrous irony: Virginia and I had come here to save one man from murder, and to help the law get its hands on the killer of three others. We now distrusted the one man acutely, and I was somewhat at odds with Aguilar who stood for the law. And I, meantime, was on passable terms with the murderer, whom I hoped to bring to justice!

I left the Stanford, our quiet little hotel, for a trip downtown. I meant to get that engagement ring, today. Virginia Trent was very English in some ways—naturally—and I figured that once she was wearing the ring it would be an irrevocable step. Not that I was afraid of losing her, but it was just a play-safe detail. And, of course, there was the sentimental side.

So I mentioned that I intended to get her ball-and-chain, kissed her with due appreciation of her spirited response, and sought a downtown-bound cable car.

Downtown I hopped off the car, having the address of a

big jewelry store, and was headed for Kearny Street when it happened: A big cheerful well-dressed man overtook me.

"Beg pardon," he said. "Are you Dr. Hugh Clements?"

"Yes," I replied in astonishment. "But how—"

"Never mind—you were pointed out to me. This is an emergency," he said. "Here's my card—Dr. James Smythe. I've been working on a former patient of yours: old chap named Chaffee. The case has me absolutely stumped. I had to give up and shoot some dope into him to keep the muscles relaxed until I could get you. Frankly, I think he's on the way out, but I understand you have used a peculiar technique that may save him. Will you come along and see him? I've a car here."

A strange thing to happen on the street of a strange city where I was unknown. But Lajpat Rai had kept me tailed, of course.

"Yes," I said. "As a physician, I can't well refuse your appeal."

"Fine!" he exclaimed, beaming. "Then hop in the car and we'll talk en route."

A car with a uniformed driver drew up at the curb, and we got in.

"This is my own car, Clements." Smythe spoke reassuringly, but still rapidly. Evidently he was not at all sure of me. "Catching you has been fast and furious work—but I must impress one thing on you: Emergency, professional secrecy, no broadcast! Savvy? We're trying to save a life—the old fellow's life. Maybe you can succeed where I failed. But we must keep silent, say nothing to anyone. You agree?"

I looked at him, and really saw him for the first time. He was earnest, sincere, rather breathless. A good man, I thought.

"Are you acting under instructions?" I asked.

He nodded.

"Yes, by phone. I don't know who gave them. At first I thought it was all screwy, until I got downtown here and you were pointed out to me—"

"Skip it," I said, and leaned back. "You're okay; for a moment I suspected you. Yes, I agree fully, if it concerns old Chaffee alone. He's not wanted for anything."

It began to come clear to me. Gerard Chaffee had gone under with one of his attacks. Lajpat Rai was unable to work on him, therefore had called in a good man—and I later found that Smythe was a very good man indeed—to handle him. An amazing thing was the rapidity and efficiency with which Lajpat Rai or his agents had acted. Smythe was unable to treat or understand the case but realizing the emergency had pumped morphia into Chaffee to relax him and check the paralysis. Meantime I had been tailed downtown. Smythe was rushed to pick me up and haul me into the case. Desperately fast work!

A physician—a good one—reacts to the need of professional secrecy when it is necessary to save a life. Smythe had reacted instantly; I had to follow suit, and said as much. He nodded at me.

"I was told that you'd understand, Clements. But the case isn't clear to me."

"Yes, he's asleep," I said. "After this Dr. Smythe will be able to treat him…. Something wrong with your arm?"

"No. I'll clear it up in a jiffy. I'm working in connection with Government men," I said, stretching things a bit, "to locate the man behind this Gerald Chaffee—the one who gave you the instructions. So I can agree, therefore, to hold the affair confidential. I'll explain the case to you."

I went on to tell how I had just returned from seven years of work in India—from long before the war, indeed—how Gerard Chaffee had been on my boat, and I had been called in when the old boy had an attack. I knew the symptoms. Chaffee had undergone torture in Tibet, being bound lengthily in certain positions which included a later muscular and nerve paralysis. My acquaintance with such things, my experience, told me what to do and so forth.

Smythe listened to my story with intent interest.

"It clears," he said at last. "They must have kept you under close surveillance to be able to put the finger on you so rapidly."

"Too damned close," I agreed. "Probably foreseeing this very contingency. In fact, I foresaw the possibility myself." I said nothing to him, of course, about Howard Chaffee, brother of the invalid. "Frankly, I don't know if I can pull the old boy through, but we'll have a try.... What the hell! Are we going *here?*"

The car was pointing up the grade for the Fairhill—the old aristocratic hotel on Nob Hill.

Smythe assented.

"Right. I'm the hotel physician. Chaffee has a room here, all alone."

This was a facer; but evidently Lajpat Rai was playing quite safe. He had put Chaffee here and was himself somewhere else—very much somewhere else. His vital interest in keeping the old fellow alive was not at all charitable. He intended to make use of him in pursuing his dream of vengeance upon Howard Chaffee; he had told me so himself.

WE WERE out of Smythe's car, without delay, then down a corridor and into a fine airy room where a nurse met us.

"Miss Simms, hotel nurse—Dr. Clements," Smythe snapped. "How is he?"

"Asleep. Relaxed. Heart not affected."

Old Chaffee, wrinkled and scarred and twisted, lay naked under a sheet. The drug had relaxed him, but any sedative was dangerous, purely an emergency measure; the nerve ganglia, I found, were still tight, and I said so.

"There's no cure, merely temporary relief," I told Smythe. "Your sedative has halted the paralysis; enough to stop the action would kill him. I'll work over the ganglia and loosen 'em up, and he'll sleep for a bit."

"How long does your relief last?" he queried, as I fell to work kneading and massaging the ganglia.

"Maybe a week or two, maybe less—can't say."

Between us, we gave that scarred, half-moribund old body a thorough going-over. While we were at it, the phone rang. The nurse answered and summoned me. I knew who it was even before I heard that remarkable voice with the timbre of a bronze bell.

"Hello, Dr. Clements! And how is Chaffee? Will he pull through?"

"I think so, Your Highness," I said with irony.

"I'm glad you're there. Could you consent to run over to see me, when you've finished with him, on similar conditions?"

"No. On no conditions whatever," I replied—and he laughed.

"Very well. I respect your honesty. Then I'll come and see you."

He rang off. I hung up and returned to work, giving Smythe a nod.

"Remarkable voice," he said. "I could hear it. Any call for police?"

"Unfortunately, no," I answered. "Evidence, warrants and such things are not yet in the picture."

"Too bad; I hoped for excitement. See here, d'you mind if I

run downstairs to my office to check on calls? Not be gone long. I'll leave Miss Simms in case you need her."

I had no objections, for he was of no great help to me. So he departed, and I worked away, in no good humor. What if Lajpat Rai did have the impudence to show up here? I could not have him arrested. There was no evidence against him to justify that extreme. Aguilar had no warrant. Certainly it was not my business to let Howard Chaffee know where his brother was, either. I must just lie doggo, and it irked me tremendously.

The job was finished at last. I stepped into the bathroom, washed my hands, and came back into the room turning down my shirtsleeves. My eye caught sight of the telephone on the dresser; a scratchpad was attached to it, and a number was penciled on the pad—*Burl. 8397.* Easy to memorize.

A knock at the door, I called to enter, and the door opened to admit Lajpat Rai.

He smiled and walked in—handsome, assured, his small black mustache setting off his golden skin. One arm was under his coat, and the sleeve dangled.

"Good afternoon," he said, throwing a glance at the nurse, who was putting the bed to rights. "I thought it needless to be announced. He's asleep, Clements?"

"Yes. May stay so for a while," I said. "After this, Dr. Smythe will be able to treat him.... Something wrong with your arm?"

"Unfortunately, yes. Useless for the time being." He smiled at me. He had stopped a bullet at Santa Barbara after murdering Balfour, but we did not mention the matter.

"Where's Dr. Smythe's office, Miss Simms?" I asked, and when she told me: "You might run along, and tell him I'll stop in on my way out."

LAJPAT RAI made no objection, and she departed. He closed the door behind her, and turned to me.

"Really, Clements, I appreciate your being here," he said quietly, earnestly. "I fully understand all it means. But there's one thing I had to ask you. Do you consider it your duty to inform Howard Chaffee where his brother is located?"

"No," I replied. Now as always, he fascinated me. His tailored tweeds, his entire getup, was immaculate. "I don't fancy your Howard Chaffee."

"Right. He'd murder this poor old devil like a shot," said the other. "Yet you are very anxious to protect him from me."

"Not at all," I replied. "Let him do that for himself. I want only to see you brought to justice as the murderer of my friend Sir James Trent."

"Because you desire to marry his daughter," he said, showing white, even teeth in a smile. "Well, that's natural. I regret it, but can't help it. If I were melodramatic and so forth, I might threaten the young lady and bring you to your senses. I shan't do that; I've nothing against her, or against you. Indeed, I shall prove as much."

I looked at him, without response. I wondered if he could feel that in my most secret heart I almost sympathized with him. After all, he fancied that a foul wrong had been done him in the past; he had every reason to seek vengeance, according to his own warped reasoning.

"No, we have different viewpoints," he said, quite as though reading my thoughts. "A pity. Well, at a previous meeting I told you that I was wealthy, powerful, impervious to any harm from you. You must have realized that was true, Dr. Clements. You cannot even find me. So I have no intention of bribing you. But you have helped this old man, who is necessary to my plans, and I am grateful. I am leaving an evidence of my gratitude at your hotel; do not reject it—it is merely a commercial object."

He turned to the door, paused, and gave me an amused glance over his shoulder.

"Your friend Mr. Aguilar," he observed, "might like to know that the papers with which I entered this country were not forged. The English consul here can no doubt obtain evidence of this fact. Good day."

He opened the door and departed. This final shot left me staring and entirely confused. What did he know, what did he guess, about Aguilar's activities? Once more I was left with the impression of his singular force it was as though the rest of us were using pea-shooters against a man in armor.

With this sense of futility, I was slipping into my coat when Smythe knocked and stepped into the room.

"Oh! Gone, is he? Remarkable fellow, Miss Simms says. I'll have her keep an eye on the patient. Anything to suggest?"

I glanced at Chaffee. "No. He's a tough old bird and can probably prescribe for himself quite safely. I'll be getting along home."

In no mood now for buying a ring I went back to the Stanford, inquired for Virginia, found her gone out. The clerk handed me a plain sealed envelope, and I remembered the words of Lajpat Rai. Opening it, I found a small envelope inside, and in this something that I turned out on my palm, amazedly.

A diamond—if it were genuine—a nice-looking one of about two carats. Or some similar stone. It looked quite blue, and

As he stepped into his car, I had a good look at him, and thought nothing of it; then I remembered something.

puzzled me. Just a commercial object, Lajpat Rai had said. An imitation stone, perhaps? With that man, anything was possible. Hm! I was not inclined to moon around the hotel all afternoon with Virginia gone. So, impulsively, I hopped a cable car and went back downtown. This was not consistent with my former mood, but a man in love is never consistent.

The gem expert tucked his glass in his eye and said: "Nice stone!"

"Yes. What kind of stone?" I asked. "That's what I want to know."

"There aren't more than three or four in the country," said he. "Blue diamond."

I had already thought about Virginia. Women are funny about engagement rings; usually they do not like any other thoughts attached to them. And this stone was from the man who had killed Sir James Trent. So I scratched the notion, bought an expensive engagement ring and turned in the blue diamond on the price.

Regaining the hotel, I found Parr sitting in the lobby, a bag between his feet. I took him up to my room, we had a drink, and talked. He liked Chaffee no more than we did, but he wanted to get the murderer of his old master, Colonel Magruder.

"What *I* like doesn't matter, sir! Unless you advise against it, I'll take my place with Mr. Chaffee and be doing my bit. Isn't that the likeliest way of getting a shot at this 'ere bloody Rajah from Hell?"

"It is," I asserted, and reaching for the phone, called Howard Chaffee's number. He answered in person and I gave my name.

"Parr's here and wants to get busy. I gathered yesterday that you want him."

"Oh, right!" said Chaffee. "Pop him in a taxi, send him here, and I'll take care of him. If he's after action, he'll get it."

"He'll be along, then. I suppose you were joking when you spoke of wanting the address of our friend from India?"

"Eh? Who—oh, come now, Clements! Pulling my leg, are

you? Joking? I'd give a thousand dollars cash on the nail to know where he is!"

"Well, his phone number is Burlingame 8397. That ought to be enough for you."

I hung up, catching Parr's eye and laughing.

"Is it really, sir?" he asked eagerly.

"I'm not sure, but I think so," I said. "He's too sharp to be caught, however."

Parr was on the scent, though; his one purpose in life was to meet this Lajpat Rai in the flesh. It had become an obsession. I saw him into a taxi, sent him off to Chaffee's house, and got back to my room to find my phone ringing. My colleague Smythe was on the line.

"Clements? Good! From the way you spoke this afternoon, I imagined you'd much like to know the address of that chap—Chaffee's friend, you know. I had him tailed when he left the hotel, and I just got a report. He went to the Burlingame Arms, a hotel in Burlingame, just south of the city. He's there under the name of Senhor Arenas—supposedly he is an Argentine businessman."

I thanked him warmly hung up and swallowed hard. My guess had been a good one.

For a crowded moment I sat thinking. Lajpat Rai must have written down that phone number for old Chaffee; he had been in the room with me, must have noticed or recalled it; he was too clever to miss such a detail. However—

I got Aguilar on the line.

"Just on the point of calling you," he said cheerfully. "I'd like to make a deal with you, Clements. Your remarks about two Chaffees—"

"All right; it's a bargain," I said. "Come along to lunch tomorrow, and we'll talk. But here's something you may be able to use, if you work fast: Lajpat Rai is at the Burlingame Arms hotel in Burlingame under the name of Arenas—presumably an Argentine capitalist. I doubt if he'll be there long. Also, the papers under which he entered this country as Hari Lal were not forged."

"Eh? How d'ye know that?"

"He told me so himself, an hour or two ago; said you might like to know."

With this parting shaft, I rang off with the Immigration man cursing me.

CHAPTER III

I WAS NOT at all proud of myself nor I of my actions as a phone relay man; my share in apprehending Lajpat Rai was minor. And it would be fruitless. He was not one to be so easily caught, or even found. I had a feeling of contempt for Howard Chaffee. With Aguilar it was different—but I could not feel sure about him.

I said something of this when I took Virginia out to dinner and a bit of dancing at one of the nightclubs on the Esplanade, the beach at the far west side of town, that evening. She nodded at me.

"I know, Hugh. How much worse do you suppose I feel—a woman, futile, doing nothing? But really, I think you're doing a lot. I'm glad you're not a beast on the hunt like our Chaffee friend; that's my impression of him."

I nodded. Having told her about Gerard Chaffee and Lajpat Rai's idea of using him against his brother, and the afternoon's events, I went into the more inviting topic of diamonds. My ring was approved, and while we were dancing I slipped it on her finger. Her protests died in admiration. We had a very pleasant evening, all in all and got back to the hotel to find a curt note in my box. It read:

"You were right—but the bird flew the nest. —A."

Anxious to see me—so anxious that he had come to the hotel instead of waiting till the morrow! I chuckled. Aguilar was where I wanted him now; no more stand-off plays! And Lajpat

Rai had skipped from the Burlingame Arms, as expected. So Chaffee had drawn blank also....

Next day was Sunday. In the morning, Virginia and I went to church, and came back to find Aguilar on hand. We settled down in a corner of the empty lobby.

"I've made discoveries," he said in his placid way. "Overnight, the whole state of things has changed amazingly. A special warrant is on the way from Washington, and I've been given charge of the case. You'd never guess why."

"I don't intend to guess," I said cheerfully. "You come clean, Mister."

HE CHUCKLED and burnished his spectacles.

"So you were talking with him yesterday! Clements, I'll come clean. To satisfy me, first tell me whether he has a slight scar on his upper lip."

I mentally pictured the handsome, powerful features of Lajpat Rai, and nodded.

"Yes. It's barely visible under the small black mustache, but it shows."

"That settles it; he's our man." Aguilar sighed contentedly and relaxed. "A man of a hundred identities! The one we want is Colonel Nicholas Myedin, so-called. Posing as a secret agent for China, he pulled some funny tricks on our Burmese forces at the close of the war. The specific charge is murder and theft of papers—a few weeks ago one of the officers engaged in the Bikini bomb tests was killed and his reports were taken, by Myedin. This is sacredly confidential, understand."

"And this Myedin is our Lajpat Rai?" I asked.

"Absolutely. Luckily, he thinks I'm only an Immigration inspector."

I was dazed. "Do you imply that he's a secret agent for China?"

"No, no! Of course not. A freelance. The man's an electrical wizard, Clements; he's now engaged in selling some amazing electronic devices to the Scott-Ames people of Vancouver, but he's not tied up with them. Scott, the head of the firm, is now here in the city. We've warned him and he sniffs; you know how Canadians can sniff. Like the British."

"I see. Chaffee got you into this game. Does he suspect that you—"

"That I'm a Federal agent? Nobody does," Aguilar said earnestly. Howard Chaffee was a dope-smuggler out of India and China. He's in with a bad crowd here—and I mean *bad!* He probably has half a dozen guns working for him right now— killers, the worst kind."

This was a new light on the leathery Chaffee. Things were opening up.

I talked—and kept nothing back. Now Lajpat Rai stood in a new light entirely, with murder as his business; I kicked myself for my sneaking sympathy with him. He had lied like a Trojan in all he had said to me. He had not been framed at all in India; he had just been caught, whatever he might fancy about injustice.

"If I'd given you quicker information yesterday, you'd have got him," I said. "You didn't like to talk, so I didn't know the truth—"

He grilled. "Too many miss because they like to talk. I don't."

"Well, the whole situation now stands in a new and clearer light. Colonel Nicholas Mycedin, eh? Then you don't care about Miss Trent's laying any charge against him in connection with her father's murder."

"I most certainly do," Aguilar said quickly. "The more charges the better. I'm not inclined to pass up any bets. He's slippery, and has a mean record."

I liked John Aguilar still more.

We decided to eat, and Virginia said she was dying to visit Fishermen's Wharf. At this, Aguilar shrugged.

"You've heard too much loose talk," said he. "It's a trap for sucker tourists who believe anything. Oh, well, there are one or two very good places there, so come on."

We took a taxicab, and had an admirable fish dinner, because Aguilar knew his way around and everyone knew him. He was a contradictory fellow even in looks, never to be taken on face value.

After the meal, he left us, intent on business. Virginia and I decided to walk alone; she loved long walks. My thoughts were naturally on Lajpat Rai—or Nicholas Myedin, as he had now become. A strange man, there; a freelance treading the verge of dizzy heights, strangely alone, strangely capable, holding murder a game to be played with huge zest!

Virginia and I did not discuss him. She wanted to see the city's unfamiliar places; we took little streets, all hill and dale, seeing the sort of landscapes that any city can produce in its meaner aspects.

Of course we missed our way and went far astray, which mattered noting. We found incredible shops, crazy streets, odd corners among those steep hills. And as we climbed one short street of little apartments, mostly with garages beneath them, I saw a man putting away his car. He opened the garage doors, got into his car, and drove it in. I had a good look at him, and thought nothing of it; then as we came to the next corner I remembered something.

His face—a kindly, aged, white-mustached face, the face of an old Hindu. The face of the old servitor of Lajpat Rai I had seen in his Los Angeles quarters weeks ago before Sir James Trent was murdered.

"Turn back, Virginia," I said, "Cross the street and turn back down—I want to get the number of a house. And what's the name of the street?"

We walked down past the garage; on the steep slope the ground floors were garages or walled, so we were below the casual sight of anyone in the house. "Thought I saw someone I knew," was my light explanation. "Evidently wrong about it." Virginia paid little attention, so I got what I wanted: 742 Colsax Street. With that address buzzing in my head, we finished our long walk.

Thinking it over, I was less sure. Perhaps mistaken recognition; perhaps merely someone who looked like the old Hindu. If that old chap were here with a car, then Lajpat Rai was here—a most unlikely and improbable thing, indeed. I was shaken, and lost confidence. Our man was a swaggering patron of great hotels and elegant hostelries, not a dweller in a hide-out in a dingy street of little flats.

So reason argued me into uncertainty; I dared take no chances on mistakes. The thing pestered me mentally all night. Go back there afoot and hang around? No, no! The whole street, except the spot immediately in front, was commanded by the house windows. I had to make sure.

VIRGINIA WAS to devote most of the day to a hair-dresser, so I felt quite free. Midmorning saw me on Colsax Street, comfortably in the back of a taxicab. The driver halted on the hillside opposite 712, left the cab, and mounted to two different entrances in search of a mythical Horace Green who had sent in a call. He did a lot of talking and gained me quite a bit of time in which to keep an eye on 742 from my hiding-place, for I had wisely taken him into my confidence.

I saw nothing significant; that two-story apartment looked deserted, the windows remained empty, no one appeared in sight. But, when my driver returned, he settled under his wheel, started the car up the hill, and nodded at me.

"No rooms to rent around here at all," he reported. "Couldn't find out who lives in 712, neither; but I did learn the place had been sold about a week ago. That help you any?"

"Not particularly," I replied. "But if you want an extra ten-spot, come back here tonight or tomorrow, do some more gossiping, and let me have early details you can pick up about the people in 742—what they look like and so forth. Anything at all."

He said "okay," and took me back to the Stanford. I was by no means satisfied and yet not thrown off the track by what I had just learned. Rents being what they were, it was not unlikely that Lajpat Rai would buy a place, money being no object to him. And yet my notion might be all moonshine, so I had to go slow, until I obtained something definite by way of evidence. And if I got it, I did not intend to take it to Chaffee. Aguilar was now in position to handle our man to more effect.

Chaffee phoned me that afternoon.

"I keep my promises, Clements," he said. "There's a check for you in the mail, a thousand. You had the goods on the guy, but I went there with Parr too late. How did you chance on that telephone number?"

"Pure accident," I said. "I wasn't too certain about it. And I don't want your money, Chaffee—"

"Forget that stuff," he broke in. "You know that paper we found in the old book? I guess it was genuine. What you told me about my brother being alive was true—and who's behind him. A lawyer has jumped on me and it looks like I'm stuck; got to pay out big money. Well, that's all right; I'm trusting it'll lead me to Lajpat Rai. Parr is a good man. I'm glad to have him on the job. Hey! Hold the line, will you?"

I assented, for excitement had shrilled in his voice. After a moment of waiting, I heard Chaffee again.

"Clements? Well, I've got something. Parr just came in. He's been scouting around a hotel at Burlingame—that's where your phone number sent us. And he's learned something there. He got the license number of the Rajah's car: a Buick sedan, registered in the name of Howard Smith, at an address in Yreka—"

"What town?" I demanded.

"Yreka." He spelled it out. "That's a town north of here. Fake name and address, of course; but it's a starting point to look for here. Do you want the number?"

I took it down, with a jumpy thrill; if that car garaged at 742 Colsax Street carried this license plate 7E-24-55, then I had the answer! Chaffee vouchsafed that the number had been obtained from the hotel garage, which listed all the cars of clients. Parr, he said, had learned that the Brazilian capitalist, Arenas, had a chauffeur, name unknown, and I could guess that this was

another crafty dodge of Lajpat Rai, who never had a car registered in his own name.

"How will this thing do you any good?" I demanded.

"Any traffic cop who spots this number gets a hundred bucks,
Clements. The same reward will be out in other quarters, too.
You'd be surprised what a reward can accomplish! It may lead
to nothing in this case, but I'm betting it will turn up something good."

There was sense in what he said, in his whole attitude. After
all, he was fighting for his life. If resources had been pooled
weeks ago, as I had desired, before the Rajah from Hell reached
so many of his victims, a winning battle might have been waged
against him—and good men might be still alive.

Excited as I was over the possibilities, I had to keep away from
that Colsax Street house. One glimpse of me hanging about
would blow the game, and off would be our quarry. How to make
sure, then, in regard to the car and its license plate? Virginia, I,
Parr, Aguilar—all of us were known by sight to Lajpat Rai, and
he probably had men tailing us all. He must have a small army
working for him; but now, while he had one arm out of commis-
sion, was the time to run him down, if ever.

I was expecting Virginia back about five. Slightly before then,
Aguilar walked into the hotel and we adjourned to the cocktail
lounge.

"Accident," said he. "I merely happened to be going past and
dropped in to say hello. I suppose you know all about the legal
troubles that have descended on our friend Chaffee."

"No," I said. "He mentioned something of the sort over the
phone though. He called to give me the license number on
Lajpat Rai's car."

Aguilar smiled. "Yes, I got that, too, at the hotel. Happens
to be a last year's plate, one of the old yellow ones. The car is
undoubtedly sporting an up-to-date plate now. Parr wouldn't
be up to the mark on such details of strategy."

This was a facer; it really knocked me for a loop. I tried to dissemble my feelings and asked about Chaffee's legal troubles.

These, said Aguilar, were bad. Howard Chaffee had inherited something like a hundred thousand dollars from the estate of his dead brother Gerard. Now it seemed that Gerard was not dead at all, but was here in San Francisco and was suing for the value of the estate. And Howard Chaffee, to cover up certain frauds of his own in connection with evidence of his brother's death in Tibet, would have to settle up on the nail.

"He admitted as much," I commented. "Lajpat Rai is behind it, of course. He regards Chaffee with venomous hatred, and I don't blame him. But tell me—how the devil do you know so much detail?"

Aguilar accepted a cigarette. "My boy, we're dealing with a smart man, one of the most clever fellows alive, in Colonel Nicholas Myedin. But let me tell you that no one, whether Al Capone or a Rajah from Hell, is smart and wealthy and powerful enough to thumb his nose at Uncle Sam's law-enforcement agencies. We're dealing with a crook, a scoundrel, a murderer. No guy like that is clever enough to beat it—in the end. Cleverness won't help him—it'd take an act of God."

I had my doubts, despite everything. Lajpat Rai, or Myedin, was a shadow, a myth. Trace him through Gerard Chaffee? Aguilar merely sniffed. Try everything, he said, neglect nothing, fail at every move—but sooner or later, the end would come. Maybe through Howard Chaffee, too. Another reason to give Chaffee rope, let him play his own game....

Now Virginia arrived, interrupting us. Aguilar stayed for another drink, refused dinner, and left us. After Virginia had changed her dress, we took a cab downtown to the Palace for a sensible old-fashioned dinner at the Garden Court—a regular London atmosphere, and excellent wine. Subdued lights, soft music, perfect service combined to make it a memorable occasion.

We were halfway through the meal, when Virginia gave me a startled glance.

"I'm not sure—or yes, I am too," she exclaimed. "Do you remember the man I saw in a drugstore at Santa Barbara, just for a moment?"

I caught my breath, as I met her eyes.

"You don't mean— No, it can't be—not here, of all places!"

"Yes. To your left and behind you; the table against the wall."

I turned a little, and saw him, slim and debonair in his evening attire, the jeweled miniature of some decoration flashing on his shirt-front—Colonel Nicholas Myedin, as he actually was—Lajpat Rai, as I knew him.

CHAPTER IV

A GLIMPSE—I DARED no more, and turned to Virginia, breathless.

"Yes, that's the man! His empty sleeve is proof enough."

"Oh! That's what puzzled me; he seemed one-armed."

Her eyes flashed; I knew she was thinking of her father's murder.

"Careful, my dear," I warned. "He has seen you; therefore he knows we're here. He's no fool. Who is that with him?"

"I don't know him; a white man," she said. "Well, do something!"

"Whatever you say." I looked at her. "What?"

At this, she bit her lip. "I'm a fool, Hugh; there's nothing we can do."

"Yes, there is, but don't get hasty," I said. "If he hasn't noticed you already, he will. He wouldn't be here unless he were perfectly safe, be sure of that. The only person I know who can tag him down for keeps is Aguilar, who has a warrant for him. Making a scene or calling in the house detectives would be just so much old horse. Neither you nor I can go find a phone without attracting his direct attention; and he'd guess what for."

"Then what?" she said.

"Call our waiter, or the head-waiter, either one you see." While speaking, I wrote on the wine-list Aguilar's name and telephone-number.

Presently our waiter came and hovered above her. Virginia handed him the list, and I did the talking.

"An extra ten-spot for you if you'll make this call: Get Mr. Aguilar and tell him to come here immediately, that the man he wants is here. I am Dr. Clements. Do it fast."

No questions, no repetitions; the waiter was intelligent. He just bowed and went away.

I smiled at Virginia.

"An extra ten-spot for you: Phone Mr. Aguilar and tell him the man he wants is here. Do it fast!"

"Now calm down. Have a cigarette; don't watch him. It's a grand play if it wins, so don't spoil it."

She nodded and lit a cigarette at the match I held. I could have sworn she never again looked at that other table, yet all the while she was watching it from the corner of her eye, and reported to me. They had ordered; they were having cocktails. A wine-bucket was brought and set at one side.

Our waiter came back. Smart man! With him he brought the sommelier, as a plausible excuse for his errand, who displayed a bottle of wine to me and talked it up. I nodded and it was opened. The waiter brushed my sleeve as he leaned forward, with a glass.

"He'll be here immediately, sir," he said softly. The job was done.

FIVE MINUTES passed. When Aguilar would get here I had no idea. Virginia was looking past me, while apparently absorbed in conversation. She reached for the ashtray and spoke softly.

"He's showing something to the other man; it looks like a little clock in a case, but it's not a clock. He's turning things and explaining it. Not a radio either; too small for that. Now he has put it on the table and is turning a dial, apparently. Perhaps it is a radio. He's moving it closer and saying something—"

Her eyes widened on me. She heard it too! A curiously quiet voice came from beside me, though no one was there. It was the voice of Lajpat Rai, like the lingering note of a bronze bell.

"Good evening, Miss Trent—Dr. Clements. This is a pleasant surprise."

A gasp escaped Virginia. "Hugh! It can't be! That table is thirty feet away! It's not real—"

"It is quite real." Lajpat Rai laughed softly. "We are talking, and no one else can hear. What do you think, Clements? Magic?"

"Hardly that," I said, not loudly. Turning, I looked at him. "If it's not some trick—some walkie-talkie or electronic development—"

"Right!" said he. "Trust your shrewd, practical brain to hit the mark! Yes, a new thing in electronics and sensory vibration. In a year or so you'll see it on the market, I believe."

Lajpat, or Myedin, reached forward and touched the glinting thing like a clock that stood before him. He was laughing at his companion, whose back was to us. There was no more voice. I turned back and met the startled gaze of Virginia Trent.

"Nobody else heard," she murmured. "No one is looking, no attention was attracted! Hugh, is it real?"

"I expect it is, my dear," I replied, and reaching over, touched her cold hand. "A bit of showing off, no doubt for his companion. Yes, give him due credit; he's a past master at electronics and such things."

"He's getting up," she said. "Putting the clock in his coat pocket—"

"Are they leaving?" I asked quickly.

"No. At least, the other man isn't; apparently he's just going out for something. He's asking the headwaiter something—now he's going out—he's gone." Her eyes came back to me. "What a handsome man there's a fascination about him—terrible!"

She was badly wrought up. I glanced around. The other man sat at the table, smoking unconcernedly, evidently awaiting his companion's return.

"Good," I said, relieved. "Colonel Nicholas Myedin has been having a bit of fun, for which he'll pay presently. Let me fill your glass, my dear; the wine is good."

She nodded. I refilled our glasses. We clicked them across the table and she responded faintly to my smile. Our waiter came, replaced the bottle in its cooler, brought up another chair and laid the place.

"He said he was coming at once, sir," he said softly. "Mr. Aguilar, I mean."

I nodded to him. "Well, Virginia, we have him trapped. It'll be interesting to see how our friend Aguilar goes to work. That double-action walkie-talkie thing will be an entertaining and valuable capture, too."

"Strange that he was so open about it," she said, frowning slightly. "Almost a defiance. I don't like it, Hugh; I wish he hadn't gone out! I wish we had stopped him."

"How?" I rejoined. "Short of brute force, I don't see how. Here comes Aguilar now. Any sign of Lajpat Rai returning?"

Her gaze swept the room behind me. "No."

AGUILAR ARRIVED, wearing a tuxedo; his shirt was not fresh, he looked as usual, mussed and off trim. He spoke to Virginia, shook hands with me. The waiter drew back his chair and he seated himself placidly.

"A surprising summons, Clements, but I think I made good time," he said in his mild way. "Outside and in here are now nine agents in all; every exit is watched too. Now, if you'll— Ah!"

He broke off, looking past me. I glanced around. Myedin's companion had risen and was walking past—a chunky, efficient-looking man, a stranger to me.

"Interesting fellow," Aguilar said. "He's the French consul here in the city, an important man. Why, what's wrong?"

Our faces must have apprised him, as the appalling realization took us. The French consul! Myedin had been dining with him, entertaining him with that electronic gadget—and had skipped out to escape the net. I knew it with ghastly certainty.

"French?" repeated Virginia. "You mean that he—that Myedin is tied up with the French consul?"

"Lord, no! Probably making use of him," snapped Aguilar. "But where is he?"

"Dining with the man who just passed," I said. "Or was. He's gone now."

Between us, we acquainted Aguilar with the situation. My worst fears were too obviously true; the table where Myedin had sat was now being cleared, he was gone. In the very instant of victory we had lost our man. He had slipped away before our faces. Like a clever magician, he had bemused us with that toy of his—then vanished.

However, in this hard moment I had to admire Aguilar. He never turned a hair.

"Too bad, but you did well, Clements," he said quietly. "We're just not good enough. Next time we must do better. I can't touch that consul, of course; diplomats are inviolate, and Myedin has just made use of him."

"He had no reason to skip out," I protested. "It was mere chance that we came."

"But he saw you and took warning." Aguilar sipped his wine, then leaned over and patted Virginia's hand. "Sorry, my dear; however, I've some interesting news for you. Wait till I dismiss my men."

He lifted a hand. Two dark-clad men came from the foyer and to our table. Aguilar looked up at them.

"I was too slow, boys," he said, with unwarranted self-blame. "Send everyone away and hope for better luck next time. It's a miss."

THE TWO men went away. Aguilar hauled some papers from his pocket and produced an amazingly poor photograph or snapshot of three men in whites. He showed it to Virginia.

"Can you recognize any of these?"

"Of course. The one in the center—he has a mustache now, but he's Lajpat Rai. At least, Dr. Clements says he is. He's the man who was recently here."

Aguilar turned to me and shoved over the picture.

"That's your man, yes," I said. "What's all this about?"

"Business," said he. "Miss Trent, when your father was—er—murdered, the actual criminal was killed. He has since been identified. He was formerly a personal servant to Lajpat Rai, also to Colonel Nicholas Myedin. Tomorrow morning I'm going to ask that you sign the complaint charging Myedin with being accessory to your father's murder. Eh?"

"Of course," she responded. "That's what I've wanted to do, but you lacked any evidence."

"I think there's enough now, with what Dr. Clements can give us, to support the charge," he said. "We don't need it, perhaps, but I like to neglect nothing."

"A dozen warrants won't help you arrest Myedin unless you can find him," I said.

"True," assented Aguilar. "Too true, in fact. Tonight is an example. He laughs at us; but the last laugh is what counts most. Well, I'll come around to your hotel in the morning, if I may, and run you down to police headquarters to get the papers duly signed and so forth."

He departed. Virginia lit a cigarette and eyed me uneasily.

"I don't like it," she said, "any of it! That man isn't my notion of a proper bulldog on the trail. He's not brisk and threatening. Then there's Lajpat Rai or Myedin or whatever his name is. Why, he seemed positively frivolous, Hugh! I don't understand it at all!"

I smiled. "You've been reading detective stories, my dear. If I work all day in the lab with a microscope and blood-specimens, I don't come home at night spotted all over with gore, you know."

"That's not the same," she said.

"Precisely the same. Colonel Nicholas Myedin, bless him, has blood on his hands an inch thick, but he keeps them outwardly clean."

That must have made her think of her father. She shivered slightly, and gathered up her coat. I called for the check, and we rose. The evening had been spoiled for us; everything had gone wrong.

Still, I wondered. Lajpat Rai never took chances without a reason. Granted that the encounter with us had been unexpected, why had he appeared here with the French consul? What considered calculation lay behind it? The thought worried me. I knew the gentleman far too well to doubt there was much chance at work—except our presence. He had shown off his electronic trick with set purpose, he had dined publicly with the French consul from set purpose, and there was nothing frivolous about it either. The more I reflected on it, the more convinced I was of this fact, and it loomed with sinister force. No man deliberately risks life and liberty for a petty gain.

One pleasing thing about our little hotel was that it had the right idea about service. The morning paper, for instance, was always pushed under the door at an early hour. I wakened next morning in good time, obtained the news sheet, and hopped back into bed to read luxuriously. Later in the morning Aguilar would come for Virginia, and I would go along with them; probably much later. No use worrying over that until the time came.

The news held nothing disquieting, I remember. International affairs were not so bad; following the Bikini bomb test of July past, things had quieted down a good deal. United States and Soviet relations were on the whole doing all right, although the usual pinpricks showed a bit of tension. I glanced at a headline "Three Men Shot" and paid no attention, until suddenly the thing rose out of the printed page and hit me like a blow in the face, as I read the sub-head over the story:

THREE MEN SHOT
MYSTERY BATTLE SHOCKS
FAIRVIEW STREET

Three men were killed at 9:30 last night in what is believed to have been an echo of Indian feuds. James Parr, caretaker of the premises at 795 Fairview Street, was shot to death and two visitors, Irwan Dhas of Bombay and an elderly man named Gerard Chaffee were the victims of the shooting. No witnesses of the affray remained to tell what took place. It was possibly a tragedy of errors, since the premises are occupied by Howard Chaffee, a brother of the dead man, who last evening was out of the city....

Incredulity seized upon me as I read. Parr, good old Scotty Parr, dead! It seemed impossible. And old Chaffee, my patient—why, he was assuredly no gunman; he could barely walk, much less go in for killings! But there it was, in cold print. The story went on to play up the mystery. Neighbors had been aroused by a sudden fusillade of shots from the house, before which a car stood at the curb—a car belonging, it was later ascertained, to Irwan Dhas. What took place, no one knew. Parr had been alone in the house, presumably. It was known that he had recently come from India. Howard Chaffee could not be reached at the time of going to press.

I looked back again at the beginning of the news item. Nine-thirty! That was precisely when Colonel Nicholas Myedin had been going through his electronic antics last evening. So my wondering was answered.

He had prepared a very careful, foolproof alibi. It explained everything, except the meaning of what had happened.

CHAPTER V

I BATHED, SHAVED, breakfasted, and I was still eating eggs and bacon when Aguilar arrived. He joined me in the hotel coffee-shop, sat down with a nod and ordered coffee.

"Myedin picked himself a good alibi last night, eh?"

"Obviously. So you've seen the story?"

"Seen it?" He permitted himself a snort. "I've been working on it since four this morning, when one of my men picked it up. Within the past hour everything has been straightened out smooth as silk. Our man is a great detail worker."

"Glad you're informed," I said. "I don't see how, or why, Parr shot those two men—old Chaffee and the strange Hindu."

"He didn't," said Aguilar. "Must have been three or four gunmen on hand. They all opened up at once, boggled things a bit, and the Hindu got a crack at Parr and killed him. That, I imagine, is what actually happened; no one knows certainly. For lagniappe, as they used to say in New Orleans, there's the odd way the Hindu was dressed: in evening clothes."

I made no comment, and Aguilar related what had happened, as he figured it.

A trap, obviously. Howard Chaffee, who must have handed

out a fat lot of money at his brother's orders, had arranged for a visit from Gerard and Lajpat Rai. The trap set, he skipped out to San Jose for the night. The visitors had come, with Irwan Dhas playing the part of the Rajah from Hell. Parr had admitted them into the house and the hidden killers had blasted them. Chaffee had got rid of his poor old brother, anyhow.

"I've investigated Myedin's connection with the French consul," Aguilar stated. "He's been selling to French interests certain electronic inventions for use with hydro-electric equipment—apparently quite legitimate. Old Gerard Chaffee left a will leaving everything he owned to the French consul here, too. Consulate lawyers have produced the will and established the claim."

A diamond or similar stone— it puzzled me. Just a commercial object, Lajpat Rai had said.

"Behind that false front, Myedin collars the money?" I said. Aguilar nodded.

"Right. All legitimate enough, of course. The man's infernally clever."

"Has Howard Chaffee come back to town?"

"Oh, sure. He's being grilled, but there's nothing on him to prove he laid any trap, of course. He remains blandly innocent."

"And can't you make any arrest?"

"No. We've no reason to touch the French interests, of course. Howard Chaffee thinks himself smart; he's a fool. Myedin will make some deal, probably killing him, and depart at will for fresh pastures. He's made a fat haul out of Gerard Chaffee."

"And you can't touch him?"

"Yes, if I could find him." Aguilar smiled and rubbed up his glasses. "That's my problem—finding him! I do not seek a battle of wits. My sole aim is to pounce on him, and if he resists arrests, to shoot."

"Simple," I commented ironically. Poor old Chaffee from Tibet! He had been no more than a pawn. He had deserved a better fate.

"Do you think Miss Trent is ready to go?" Aguilar asked. "We'd best get off."

"I don't know," I said discourteously. "Look her up yourself."

HE LEFT to do so; I paid the check and stepped outside for a breath of fresh air, feeling morose and shocked. Parr's death left me much disturbed, too. In passing the desk I took an envelope that was shoved at me as my mail. After a few moments I opened it.

The sole contents was a check for a thousand dollars, signed by Howard Chaffee—the money he had said was in the mail. I stood there in the sunlight, staring at it, then abruptly tore it into scraps and stepped over to the gutter, throwing away the pieces. I wanted none of his money. It was no less than an insult.

"Hey, there! Hey, Mister!" said a voice. "It's me!"

I glanced around. A taxi had drawn up at the curb almost beside me. There was a face I recognized, grinning at me. With a rush, I remembered the taxi-man I had sent to pick up anything he could at the Colsax Street house. He had slipped clear out of my mind with the rush of events.

"Oh, hello!" I said, and opening the cab door, got in. "Stick around; we'll be needing you in a few minutes. Get anything on that house?"

"Yeah, but I been sick," he replied. "I sent a couple kids around there to scout. They done a good job. Only person they seen was an old guy, dark-complexioned, like a Mexican, with white mustache."

I nodded. The same man I had seen.

"Buick sedan in the garage," he went on.

I caught at the name. Lajpat Rai had used a Buick at Burlingame.

"Did they see the license number?"

"Yeah; California, but they didn't get the number—just kids, you know." He spoke apologetically. "Got something else they hauled out of a trash barrel back of the house last night. Don't know if it means anything to you or not. It's a last year's plate, of course, orange and black instead of black and white—"

He lugged forth into sight a bent, bedraggled old license plate. When I saw the orange number upon it, I think my heart stood still for an instant. The number was 7E-24-55: the number of Lajpat Rai's car at the Burlingame Arms. The car had returned to this house on Colsax Street, the old plates had been stripped off and replaced by new ones—and this was one of the old plates from a trash-barrel!

That house was the secret hideaway of Nicholas Myedin!

I fumbled some money into his hand, seized the plate and shoved it under my coat, and got into the hotel; I did not feel safe until I had reached my room and put the thing out of sight. Then I came back down and met Virginia and Aguilar, and put them into the taxicab. I begged off going along; I was not needed, and did need to sit down and think what I was to do.

It was not so easy. The obvious thing, of course, was to advise Aguilar at once and let him fall to work. To be honest, I was afraid of failure, I think. Last night's affair had unsettled me; I could picture Myedin again scenting a trap and taking to flight. I was unsure of Aguilar, and too bitterly sure of the Rajah from Hell.

Yet what else could I do? Alone, nothing whatever. I sat in my room, shaking with buck fever, unable to determine on anything. I had the positive certainty now: Our man was in that house. Gradually the conviction came to me that there was only one thing to do—put my information in Aguilar's hands and let him act upon it. This was sensible, and calmed me to realize it. Thought of Parr did urge me to tell Chaffee and let him put his gunmen to work, but this would be folly and I knew it.

MY ROOM phone rang. I picked up the receiver to hear Chaffee's voice.

"Clements? I'm down here in the bar. Can you come down? Can't stop five minutes."

"Right down," I said, and suited action to words.

I found him seated at a drink, and the sight of him was a shock. He looked ten years older, shaken, nervous.

"You've seen the papers? I've had a hell of a time with the cops and all," he snarled. "On my way home now. Just stopped in for a minute. I don't suppose you know anything—bad business last night, all of it. Well, I've had my notice."

His manner, his snarling whine, put me off any thought of confiding in him.

"Your notice? What d'you mean?" I inquired.

"Telegram, unsigned. Said all accounts would be settled inside two days," he responded jerkily. "You know what that means— same as the others. I've got to use my head now; I'm going to let that bastard come after me, and then get him for keeps. By the way, I'm sorry about Parr."

"So am I," was my reply.

That was all. He had left his car outside, and I went out to it with him.

"So long," he said. "Don't count me out yet; I'm going to get him. If you pick up anything, let me know."

I merely nodded, and he drove off. I did feel a little guilty for letting him go and saying nothing—but it was the only wise course. Aguilar was the only man to trust.

I had to pay in worry for my indecision, however. Virginia came home alone; Aguilar had been detained on some business, she said. She had learned all about last night's affair, too, and it had put her into a dither of nervousness.

I was even worse off, for I tried everywhere to get hold of Aguilar, and could not. It was three in the afternoon before he telephoned.

"You'd better get here on the jump," I said.

"No can do," he rejoined. "I've an important meeting—"

"Listen," I broke in. "I've got everything you want—*everything*, understand? I haven't told even Virginia. I'm the only soul who knows, and I won't talk over the wire. But this is the wind-up if you don't bungle it."

"Oh!" he said slowly. "All right, then. I'll be there in ten minutes."

Three minutes later my phone rang again. I answered.

"Hi, Clements. This is Chaffee. Free this evening?"

"Unfortunately, no," I answered. "But why?"

"I thought you might like to sit in on a party with me," he said. "Looks as if it would clean up this business of ours at one crack. Get me?"

"Oh!" I thought fast. "You mean you've found the fellow?"

"No. I've got him coming to me. I got a line on him and I'm using it."

"Sorry," I rejoined, in relief. The game was still mine, and I wanted none of his traps. "I'm definitely tied up, tempting as you make it sound."

"Okay—your loss," he responded, and hung up in an evident huff.

I was not worried about his reaction, but wiped my brow; for an instant he had started me sweating, with the suspicion that he had discovered about the Colsax Street house. So he had got a line on Colonel Nicholas and had laid another trap? Evidently he had not learned his lesson the first time, I reflected. A bungler; and I had been so tempted to reveal my precious secret to such a rogue!

Virginia heard nothing of the secret. Not that I distrusted her, of course; I distrusted fate. When Aguilar arrived, he came directly to my room. I let him in and pointed to a chair. He settled into it.

"Very odd thing, if you spoke the truth over the phone," he said. "Chaffee had a notion to end the game tonight, too. I was with him when I called you."

"Howard Chaffee?" I stared at him.

He nodded, calm and unexcited.

"Right. He's been lucky in a way. Remember the fellow killed last night in company with Gerard Chaffee—Irwan Dhas? Well, Chaffee found he had a brother working in a store on Dupont Street and thinks it's a direct lead to Colonel Nicholas Myedin; so he's given the fellow a message to deliver. Of course, the man swears he never heard of Lajpat Rai and so forth; I think myself he lies, and the message will be delivered. Chaffee wanted me in on it; I refused."

"Does Chaffee know you for what you are?"

He shook his head, smiling slightly. "No. I think he suspects something, though, from my pull with the cops. He's probably heard of the FBI and such organizations."

"But I don't savvy it, Aguilar! What kind of a message to our man?"

"A damn' fool one. Precisely what Myedin will most like to

hear. Chaffee is the bait; he'll be waiting in a car marked with a blue taillight at nine tonight, on the outer Esplanade drive opposite McGinty's Café. Fine deserted sea-coast at that spot. He wants Lajpat to meet him and call everything off—offers big money and so forth."

"Still I don't get it. Will he really be in the car?"

"Absolutely. He figures he's being closely watched and Lajpat will come to finish him. But he has or will have men hidden, marksmen. He gambles his life on their ability to act first."

"Damned nonsense!" I exclaimed. "It's no more than a child-ish variant of the trap he set last night—brave, if you like, but silly."

Aguilar nodded. "So I tried to argue. But that's Chaffee himself—courageous, perfectly willing to gamble his life, but nervous and shaken, unstable, at extremes. Did you get me here to receive news, or to talk my head off?"

"Oh! Excuse me," I said quickly. "The point is, Chaffee called me and offered to let me in on the party, just after you had left him."

"He talks too much." Aguilar made a nervous gesture. "I think Myedin will copper him tonight, somehow. That fellow

*When I saw the number upon it, I think my heart
stood still for an instant—Lajpat Rai's old number!*

smells a trap afar off. I'd not want to be in Chaffee's boots at nine tonight."

He sat looking at me. A muscle twitched in his cheek; he was actually nervous as hell and trying to keep it hidden. I smiled at him.

"Oh, you want information! Very well. The Rajah from Hell is living at 742 Colsax Street, apparently with only one servant."

Aguilar blinked. "Guesswork?" he said.

I reached out the license plate. "This is real, solid fact. Finger it. I'll tell you the whole thing, and you can draw your own conclusions."

So, unhurriedly, I began with the car at the Burlingame Arms, told how my attention had fallen upon the Colsax Street house, and what had happened since. Through it all, John Aguilar listened in utter silence, eyes fastened upon me, until I had finished. He looked blank, emotionless, stony.

"I see," he said at last. "You've been careful. Good work, Dr. Clements. Very pretty work indeed." He stirred and rose. "I must be off."

"Eh?" I said, surprised. "Off? Where?"

"To find a taxicab and have a look at that house myself, now, in the full light of day. Our man's there, no doubt of that. We'll smoke him out tonight—unless Chaffee gets him first. We'll do it, in fact, while Chaffee is springing his little silly trap."

CHAPTER VI

AGUILAR GOT his look around, which of course showed him only a blank house. To my surprise, however, he showed up with a city survey of the district, showing everything in and about each lot.

He advised saying nothing to Virginia, and I agreed. She would necessarily have worried keenly. Besides, he wanted to keep the facts known only to the two of us; like me, he feared lest the Rajah from Hell could pick secrets from out of the very air. And he could just about do that with his electronic apparatus, too.

Aguilar showed up for dinner with us at the hotel. I told Virginia I was going out with him later to hold a conference upon the whole business, and she asked no questions. In fact, we left immediately after dinner; Aguilar had a car, and drove downtown on Post Street to a bungalow that served him for living-quarters and office. He had a bare, homeless sort of place there. His office had nothing in it except a big city map on the wall, an ancient roll-top desk, three telephones and a couple of chairs.

"Well, it's seven-thirty—loads of time." Aguilar took a creaky chair at the desk and began to load a pipe. Before he had it lighted, the phones began to ring; he got five calls within two minutes. To each one he replied just three words:

"Nine o'clock. Okay."

He hung up finally and grinned at me. "Military dispositions, Clements. This time, no mistake; everything covered. Even so, I expect he'll spring something on us at the last minute; maybe he'll vanish into thin air."

A sour jest—too apt to come true.

"Nine o'clock?" I said. "That's precisely when Chaffee has set his trap. Aren't you going to stop that foolishness?"

"No. It's very opportune for us," said Aguilar, smoking comfortably. "It's a long way from that house over to the Esplanade; gives us plenty of time to operate."

"Suppose the trap works and Chaffee kills him?"

He shrugged. "I'll not mind. I've given up all hope of catching him alive."

"And if Chaffee is killed?"

"No particular loss, as I look at it," he returned calmly. "Might even be a distinct gain. Anyhow, the thing distracts our man's attention."

"If he goes himself," I added. "He may not."

"We'll know before we leave here," said Aguilar. I gave him

a sharp inquiring glance but he vouchsafed no information. Apparently he wanted to divulge none of his preparations, and I blamed him not a bit.

IT WAS a dismal hour that we put in, so far as I was concerned. We smoked, talked, got occasional phone reports. Eight-thirty came. Aguilar rose, opened a closet, and came out with a long walkie-talkie outfit. I helped him get it on his back.

"Expect to use this thing—in a city?" I demanded.

"The Signal Corps has developed it for that express purpose, my skeptical friend. We're going to fight the Rajah from Hell with his own weapons— Ah!"

A buzz; he made answer, listened, stood there smiling, and cut off.

"We'd better go, Clements. The Buick sedan is just leaving the Colsax Street garage now," he said. "Two men in it—Myedin himself is on the job. And for the first time, he's made a mistake, a serious one. Never mind; you'll see when we get there. My car has a driver; come along. You have a gun?"

I nodded, and we left the bungalow. Outside, a driver was in his car. We got in and the car started. Aguilar had to sit hunched over because of the walkie-talkie; from time to time, he got reports. To Colsax Street was only a short distance. When we turned into it, we drove past the house without stopping. The garage doors were closed. A floodlight at the top of the steps illumined them brightly; no one could approach the house from the street below without being distinctly visible.

"That's his mistake," said Aguilar softly. Our car stopped at the curb slightly up the street and opposite. "Plenty of light there—none in back! And it's possible to get at the house from the rear. Keep your eye on the place, now; we're running on schedule."

I looked, and saw not a soul in the street, though down the block two or three cars stood at the curb. A small car came toiling up the hill and stopped before 742. A man got out and started up the stairs that climbed to the house. In that floodlight every detail was visible. He wore a telegraph messenger's uniform and cap. A telegram for Colonel Nicholas Myedin, no doubt. He was all alone. No one else was in his car.

It was close to nine o'clock, almost upon the hour, in fact.

I watched those lighted steps, and saw no one. The house entrance itself was of course invisible from the street. Suddenly there came a buzz from Aguilar's contraption; he answered, listened, then spoke.

"Okay.... Here, Clements! Help me off with this thing."

In the confined space, it was a job getting the straps unbuckled and off. As he got clear, he told me:

"As we expected: Chaffee's parked car was just smashed to flinders by another car. Not the Buick, of course; Myedin was too smart for that—probably had another car all set for the job. No details yet, of course. Well, that finishes Chaffee; now we'll have to step on it. All right, Charley; come along with us."

The driver hopped out as we left the car, and I caught the bulge of a holster at his belt. Aguilar led the way, and as we crossed the street, the figure of the messenger came down the

"Okay, boss," said a composed voice.
"Just like clockwork. Got him."

lighted steps, fast, got into his car and shoved off. We were going up those lighted steps almost before he was gone.

So Howard Chaffee was probably done for! Twice he had set a trap and caught the wrong prey. Well, he had been warned. I had no doubt that he was dead, when Lajpat Rai struck, he did not waste his blows. And what were we walking into, here in this blaze of light where anybody up above could see us clearly? Perhaps Aguilar suspected my hesitation.

"Step fast, Clements!" he said. "If the messenger got anyone in the house to answer the door, it's all right. If not, it isn't."

Our chauffeur dashed ahead of us, a flashlight in his hand. We were at the top, and out of the floodlight. Ahead was darkness and movement and the stabbing beam of the flashlight.

"Okay, boss," said a composed voice. "Just like clockwork. Got him."

Understanding broke upon me: The messenger was a decoy. Here under the ray of light was Lajpat Rai's servitor, the gentle, kindly old man whom I knew by sight. He was now handcuffed and between two other men who held him. They had come in from the rear, to the house.

"Good work," Aguilar said. "Inside with him somewhere, out of the way. Tie him in a chair and gag him. Make sure that he touches nothing. Charley, take a look through the house. Careful not to touch anything."

He had a small flashlight and signaled with it, as the others moved into the house, which was all dark. I caught two answering stabs of light from the bushes around; more men were stationed there. The little entrance porch where we stood was in inky darkness.

"I think, Doctor," said Aguilar, "we'd better stop right here. Catch him in the entrance; a flashlight is always very startling. He may double back for the street, and then my men down below will have him trapped on the stairs."

" 'Him?' There'll be another man with him," I said. "Two men left here."

"Yes, of course. I wonder why? Must be a reason," he said musingly. "Well, we'd better shut up. He's a bit overdue now. We'll have warning when he comes into the garage; we can hear the doors."

We waited a long while; everything was black, everything was still. A dog in the adjoining yard began to bark, but roused no response and desisted. Deceptive as the minutes were, I knew they were flitting steadily away. To get here from the Esplanade, with a good driver, should take no more than ten minutes, with luck. Much more than that had elapsed since the report of the crash had come in on the walkie-talkie.

The porch on which we stood was only a step above the ground and was surrounded by a low half-rail a couple of feet high. The house door was standing wide open. I caught a brief ray of light in the hall and heard a footstep. The light struck us and vanished.

"It's me," said the voice of our driver, Charley, who was undoubtedly one of Aguilar's men. He spoke under his breath, cautiously: "House is empty. Lot of scientific apparatus in one room. One of the upper rooms projects and has a full view of the street below, and the steps up, in that blaze of light."

"Scram," said Aguilar. "And quick about it."

A S H E spoke, I heard a car door slam, and the sound prickled in every nerve. Charley disappeared silently. I listened for the scuff of feet on the cement steps, but could hear nothing Then, causing a distinct shock that was almost panic, an electric light over our heads flashed on, bathing the entrance in light.

I met the staring, startled gaze of Aguilar. I must have looked still more wide-eyed, for a shadowy smile came to his lips. He pointed down, and I understood. Someone in the garage, below, must have turned a switch. It was as simple as that. Colonel Nicholas Myedin had come home, and the trap was sprung.

No doing anything about it, of course. I questioned Aguilar with a look, and he shrugged. After all, it did not matter. If Myedin got this far, he was caught, and the light would merely prevent any attempt at escape. So, producing a cigarette, I lighted it and we waited. Now we could hear the sound of footsteps. Aguilar quietly stepped to the house door and pulled it nearly shut. Everything was strangely prosaic. Our anticipations had been absurd; there was no flourish of pistols, nothing melodramatic—just a man walking into the trap.

It seemed almost a pity, I thought, that the Rajah from Hell should end up in so tame and unglamorous a fashion. For he had no earthly chance of evasion or escape. Men inside the house, around it, men down below closing in upon him—

The footsteps were closer now. A voice was murmuring low words; I caught the metallic timbre of the voice I knew so well. A figure moved at the edge of the light. I flipped away my cigarette; no further need now of any concealment. Then I stood petrified, as the approaching figure came into the light with a sudden cry and a quick step forward.

"Oh, Hugh! He—he said you'd be here—"

It was Virginia Trent.

CHAPTER VII

THERE WAS an instant of stupefied silence.
I stared past Virginia, as I folded an arm about her, and saw Lajpat Rai standing there, within the circle of light. His guard was down; he looked utterly astounded as he regarded us. Virginia was speaking rapidly.

"He said you were here, that you wanted me; I thought it was a lie, but I couldn't refuse to come—he was very polite—"

Lajpat Rai broke into a laugh, and stepped forward.

"A delicious irony," he said. "Yes. I did say you were here; I meant to get you later, Clements, and somehow arrange with both of you an end to hostilities. And here you are! Evidently I was right in suspecting that your continued enmity would be perilous. I disregarded you too long."

But before I could speak, Aguilar stepped out.

"Here you're not dealing with Dr. Clements, but with me. Colonel Nicholas Myedin, I have a warrant in my pocket. You're under arrest for murder; I counsel you to make no attempt to escape. I have men covering you this moment."

"Indeed! Mr. Aguilar, I believe." Myedin surveyed him with arrogance, seemed about to go on speaking, then checked himself abruptly. Pride, perhaps, or vanity. His trim figure, with one sleeve dangling, looked grotesque.

"Your hand, please," Aguilar commanded. I saw that he held a pair of handcuffs. Myedin saw it also, and started slightly.

"No," he said, a flat statement, a positive refusal. "You should add kidnap charges to your fantastic list. Or don't you suppose I kidnapped Miss Trent?"

"Oh, don't be silly!" broke out Virginia. "He didn't at all, really. I came quite voluntarily; everything was very pleasant!"

Myedin bowed to her. "Thank you, Miss Trent. May I suggest that things might be more comfortable all around if we stepped into the house?"

Tumult, darkness, men stumbling into one another—then, suddenly a frightening burst of red flame erupted in our faces.

"No!" I exclaimed sharply. All eyes went to me. "Careful, Aguilar! He's an expert illusionist. You've forgotten one important thing: two men left this house—where's the other one?"

I had hit the mark; Myedin's face told me as much. Then he stepped forward past us to the doorway and paused, turning.

"Nonsense!" he exclaimed cheerfully. "These charges are fantastic. If Mr. Aguilar really has a warrant, I demand to see it. Come inside, and let's go at the thing reasonably. I shan't refuse to accompany you to police headquarters if you insist; naturally, I'm not fool enough to resist, since I can clear away all accusations in no time—"

He spoke rapidly, genially, giving no one any chance to object. As he spoke, he put out his one hand and shoved the door open. It all happened rapidly after I had cried out my protest, too swiftly for other action. And as he pushed open the door, he found a switch inside and clicked it.

The light here was extinguished; we were plunged into pitch darkness.

Noise—alarmed voices burst forth everywhere. I pulled Virginia to one side and held her close. Men came rushing upon the porch from every side. Aguilar, I think, reached the switch and the light returned, to show Myedin gone—into the house, of course. A pistol exploded somewhere inside, and at this everyone was shoving in. I abandoned Virginia and pushed in with the others, furious and aghast at the happening.

Tumult, darkness, men stumbling into one another, flashlights stabbing long rays of light across the rooms, everything in confusion—and then, so suddenly that it frightened us all, a burst of red flame erupting in our faces. How or why, we knew not. Half a dozen shots roared out; then we were frantically shoving back, away from the fierce redness—for the rooms ahead of us were alight in an instant as though the house had leaped all at once into flames.

So it had, too, doubtless made ready beforehand. For as we retreated, the fire came gushing after us in a most incredible and appalling manner. We tumbled outside—two men shot and nearly helpless, another dead and dragged forth limply. Everyone was shouting; an access of fear and horror had seized all except Aguilar, who continued shouting frantic orders. He made himself heard; the men scattered.

I REACHED Virginia, caught her hand, and we got away from the searing heat into a corner of the grounds. The house was now a pillar of spouting flame and thick oily smoke; everything was bright as day. The hurt men were brought to me— one dead, two with bullet-wounds, a couple more badly burned. Virginia and I, the only persons halfway calm, took charge and did what we could. The old Hindu servant of Lajpat Rai had apparently not been got clear.

"I think we got Myedin." Aguilar joined us, shouting above the crackling roar of flame. "Two men are positive they dropped him; they say he's still in there."

"We'd better scram before we roast to death," I responded.

This made sense. We got past a fence and into the next backyard with our wounded. The houses adjoining were already in wild commotion, with people running about like mad.

In time—it seemed a century—police and firemen arrived; by then, the house was a fiery mass past any saving. Virginia and I were taken back to the hotel in a radio car; to reenter that peaceful, serene atmosphere seemed like a dream. I was astonished to find my clothes dotted with burns. In the wild excitement I had been unaware of the damage.

An hour later Aguilar arrived. He came direct to my room and nodded as he saw my ruined garments spread out. His own were almost as bad.

"Chemicals," he said. "The damned place was a volcano, Clements!"

I poured him a drink, and he gulped it.

"Well?" I demanded. "Did you make certain about—him?"

He looked at me. "Eh? Him? Two of my men swore they got him. If so, his body is there still. He didn't get away through the cordon; they're all sure of that. We'll know later on, when the ashes can be searched. If they find no trace of him—"

They found none, though they located the old Hindu servant. This proved nothing.

Three days later Virginia and I were married and left San Francisco. The authorities were quite satisfied that the Rajah from Hell was dead.

But as for me—well, two men left that house in the Buick sedan. We saw one return. Did the other come by some unguessed route? Well, it's none of my business. I have my own life to live.

ABOUT THE AUTHOR

H. BEDFORD-JONES is a Canadian by birth, but not by profession, having removed to the United States at the age of one year. For over twenty years he has been more or less profitably engaged in writing and traveling. As he has seldom resided in one place longer than a year or so and is a person of retiring habits, he is somewhat a man of mystery; more than once he has suffered from unscrupulous gentlemen who impersonated him—one of whom murdered a wife and was subsequently shot by the police, luckily after losing his alias.

The real Bedford-Jones is an elderly man, whose gray hair and precise attire give him rather the appearance of a retired foreign diplomat. His hobby is stamp collecting, and his collection of Japan is said to be one of the finest in existence. At present writing he is en route to Morocco, and when this appears in print he will probably be somewhere on the Mojave Desert in company with Erle Stanley Gardner.

Questioned as to the main facts in his life, he declared there was only one main fact, but it was not for publication; that his life had been uneventful except for numerous financial losses, and that his only adventures lay in evading adventurers. In his younger years he was something of an athlete, but the encroachments of age preclude any active pursuits except that of motoring. He is usually to be found poring over his stamps, working at his typewriter, or laboring in his California rose garden, which is one of the sights of Cathedral Cañon, near Palm Springs.